Foxy Mysteries Book 3

Deadly

Deceit

1

The tall, lanky redhead pulled out a bar stool and took a seat at the long island bench. 'What case are you working on now?' Connie swirled her glass of wine as Liz pulled the roast chicken out of the oven and stabbed it with a long, stainless-steel skewer.

'I have a few on the go.' Liz had only been in the PI business a few months, but she'd already solved a murder and found two kidnap victims. 'Mostly boring, run-of-the-mill stuff. You know, insurance fraud, corporate extortion. I got that case from Jackie's dad believe it or not.'

Connie laughed. 'Oh, how does his *wife* feel about that?'

Liz shrugged. 'I don't think Jackie's adoptive mum knows much about anything that goes on around her to be honest. It seems there is plenty her husband doesn't tell her.' Liz winked and Connie giggled. They both knew Liz had recently done some digging and discovered her daughter's adoptive dad had been a client of her escort agency.

'Well, that new client, the one Ted referred, has his first date this Friday. I've paired him up with Amanda. He was hard work to begin with. He seemed fixated on you for some reason, but I managed to convince him you weren't taking new clients and that Amanda would look after him just as well.'

'Somehow I doubt that.' Liz flicked her hair and pouted, putting on her best sexy pose. Connie spat her wine back into her glass before allowing herself a choking laugh, a wine spill crisis, barely averted.

'You miss the escort work, don't you?' Connie asked as she lifted her glass to the light and studied her wine to make sure it was still safe to drink.

Liz shrugged. 'I'm *still* working, just not as often.'

'Ah ha.' Connie grinned as Liz began to dish up the food. 'What?'

'I've not seen a client on your personal calendar for weeks.'

Liz shrugged. 'I've been pre-occupied with my case load. Linking that kidnapping with two murders in Victoria was huge.'

'Nothing at all to do with Detective Jack Cunningham.' It wasn't a question and Liz frowned.

'In a manner of speaking yes. I've been helping figure out who tried to kill his dad, not that I think much of his father, but Jack is trying to uncover the motive. Is it related to a case the Judge tried or is it to do with his dirty dealings? The more we dig, the more we discover what Judge Bruce Cunningham has his fingers into.'

'And I'm sure the detective couldn't manage to figure it out without you and Max helping. It's not like he hasn't been a detective for over a decade or anything.'

'Oh shut up and drink your wine.' Liz refilled Connie's glass before opening the top drawer to get cutlery out. Her friend watched her closely, waiting for her to offer more, but Liz wasn't going there.

'Do you want gravy?' Connie shrugged, realising Liz was purposefully changing the subject.

'Sure, why not. How's Jackie doing anyway?' Connie let the matter go, opting for a safer subject.

'She's great, heading into her final exam period soon, so she's head down, bum up studying. Final exams will be done and dusted by September, but law is so full on, it's taking all her spare time.'

'Intense. I'm so glad I let the study go. I don't think my heart was really in it anyway.'

'Are you going okay now that you're helping me manage the agency? It's not taking up too much of your spare time, is it?'

'Stop worrying Liz. I wouldn't have agreed to come on as partner if I didn't want to do it. I'm enjoying it, really.'

Liz offered Connie her plate and walked around the wide stone kitchen island, pulling up a stool alongside her friend.

'Thanks. I don't know how I'd be managing everything without your help. Since discovering Jackie was my daughter and her wanting to spend time with me as her biological mother, then Becca's murder and getting myself sucked into that, I've been a tad overloaded.' Liz didn't often open up about her limitations, but Connie had been one of her closest friends for years—since Liz had rescued her from her abusive partner and given her work in the agency.

Connie cut a piece of chicken and layered mashed potato on top of her fork. 'I get it. You've been the madam of Foxy Escorts for over twenty years and being a PI is new and exciting. I say go for it, enjoy yourself. You've earnt it and I appreciate you bringing me in. The money is great and I'm not getting any younger, taking on new clients wasn't really an option for me anymore.'

The women both laughed. Neither of them could keep up the escort work forever. Liz was getting close to fifty and Connie was less than a decade behind.

Connie put her fork full of food in her mouth and Liz was about to do the same when her smart-watch vibrated on her wrist. She looked at the screen, recognising Max's number.

'I better get this.' She put her cutlery down and picked up her mobile which was vibrating on the large, formal dining table behind her.

'Yep?'

'Gotta love your friendly phone manner.' Max sounded agitated.

'I'm in the middle of dinner with Connie.'

'Oh, sorry. This is important.'

'Okay, what do you need?' She should have realised it was urgent. Max seldom bothered her at home, even since they'd started working together in her new investigation business. An ex-cop and her ex-husband, they were still getting used to the new arrangement.

'It's Jack. He's been arrested.'

'That's impossible. He's a senior detective, why the hell would anyone arrest him?'

'It's bad Liz. The Bikie Task Force raided his house and they *say* they found drugs. Like father, like son they said.'

'That's bullshit. How did you find out?' Liz was pacing her polished porcelain tiled floor, her Ugg-boot slippers slapping the tiles. Connie had stopped eating and was sitting on the edge of her chair, an intense frown on her face as she patiently waited to find out what was wrong.

'Jenny. She called me a few minutes ago. They've brought in Internal Affairs and pulled him and Jenny off the investigation into who poisoned his dad.'

'Of course they have. How convenient.'

'Exactly. Look, we need to meet up with Jenny. I'll contact Jack's mum and get a good lawyer organised.'

'Nope. I've got that covered. I'll make a call now. Get Jenny and meet me here first thing in the morning. I need to do some research and call in a few favours first.'

'Got it.' There was a moment of silence, and Max didn't hang up right away. 'Liz, I'm sorry. I should have seen this coming.'

'It's not your fault Max. He's your ex -partner, your friend, I'm sorry he's in trouble just as much as you are. See you at eight sharp.' Liz hung up and turned to Connie.

'Jack's in a shit load of trouble.'

2

Liz pressed the button to open her blinds. Winter was in full swing now, outside looking grey and gloomy, reflecting her mood. She flicked on the heating on her way to the kitchen, where she turned on the coffee machine.

A quick glance at her watch told her she had fifteen minutes up her sleeve, just enough time to make coffee for everyone and prepare a quick breakfast.

Opening the fridge, Liz let her mind wander. Jack under arrest. That just left a bad taste in her mouth. Of all the police officers she'd ever met, Jack was as clean as they came. He didn't even accept her buying him coffee when they met for fear of being accused of bribery. There was no way he was mixed up in any of this. A total stitch up, likely someone who wanted to keep him off his dad's corruption investigation.

The cold air falling from the fridge brought her back to reality. Collecting the butter, she put a few slices of toast on and pressed her favourite coffee selection on her automatic coffee machine.

The door buzzer sounded just as she was getting the caramel syrup Detective Williams loved so much out of the pantry. Liz leant over and checked the camera on her benchtop tablet to make sure it was who she was expecting. Two familiar faces, looked sombrely at her through the fisheye lens. Liz, caramel syrup still in hand walked over to the door and let the detective and former detective in.

'I'm just making coffee, assuming you both want one?'

'Yes please.' Jenny joined Liz in the kitchen. 'Can I help?'

'If you want some toast, then help yourself.'

6

'I've eaten, thanks. Max, you want something?' Jenny looked over her shoulder as Max pulled a stool out at the kitchen counter and slumped heavily onto the seat.

'You know me, I'm always hungry.' He forced a smile and Liz could see he'd not slept well.

'The lawyer, my lawyer, will be visiting Jack this morning. She'll have him out on bail in a flash. I can't believe they held him overnight.' Liz was still fuming.

'I haven't had a chance to speak with the chief yet. Surely he wouldn't have pushed to remand him in custody?' Jenny didn't look at all sure as she put two slices of bread in the toaster for Max.

Liz handed two coffees across the kitchen bench and started buttering her toast.

'Don't speak to the Chief Jenny. I'm not sure who we can trust right now.' Max took a sip of his coffee and wiped the froth from his lips before continuing. 'Liz knows him from way back. What do you think?'

'I think we keep our cards close to our chest. Jenny, if you can keep an eye on department gossip and Max, you and I can work our own investigation. I've already made a few calls. If the Bikie Task Force is involved, then they were tipped off by someone. We just need to find out who that someone was.'

Liz put Vegemite on her toast and took her coffee to a seat at the counter. More toast popped behind Jenny and she picked it out, put it on a plate and handed it to Max, together with the butter and a few options to top it off.

'It's pretty weird that the Bikie Task Force raided Jack's house. Why them? Is there a link to Jack's dad's case or did someone frame Jack to get him off another case? Max buttered his toast and put honey on top, so thick that it ran off the edges as he picked it up to take a bite.

'I don't know Max, but whoever it was feels more comfortable with the Task Force running the investigation, and not Jack. Or could it be related to another case Jenny?' Liz took a breath, considering the situation.

'We don't have much on at the moment, but it could be a past case?'

Liz finished a bite of toast and took a sip of coffee. 'I spoke to a former Bikie acquaintance. He said the word is that the Judge was tied up with the Harlequins outlaw bikie gang, maybe Jack figured out it was them who tried to kill his dad? They'd have the drugs handy to plant. Who would know where Jack was at in his investigation?' Liz directed the question to Jenny.

'We don't share offices with the Task Force, so no one from that department would have known what Jack was following up on. He wasn't even really sharing his investigation with me, not in detail anyway. He never mentioned bikies to me.'

'Was he the only detective in Major Crimes on it? Surely he wasn't lead on his dad's case?' Max licked the honey from his fingers and Liz threw him a hand towel, a scowl on her face. 'I'm surprised he was on the case at all.'

'He wasn't. Rickard and Johnnie were. It wasn't our case.'

'This isn't making any sense. The Bikie Task Force must have just been a tip-off, nothing to do with investigating the Judge's attempted murder, but why them? Why not regular police? We need to speak with Jack. He's stepped on someone's toes.' Liz took another sip of coffee.

'That sounds more like something *you'd* do.' Max teased Liz rolled her eyes, failing to see the funny side.

'Jenny, can you go to work today, sniff around, carefully, and see what the detectives on Jack's dad's case know so far?

Max, if you can meet Jack when he's released on bail, I'll keep digging into why the Bikie Task Force has been roped into this.'

'Be careful Liz, Bikies aren't known for their subtle warnings. If you find anything, anything at all, let me know before you make a move. The Harlequins aren't small time. They have connections to international crime gangs and they killed that detective in Western Australia with a car-bomb back in the early two-thousands.' Max looked worried as he used the towel to do a final wipe of his hands and moved towards the door, Jenny joining him.

'I'll be careful this time Max. I promise.'

'You better be Liz. This isn't amateur detective hour. The Harlequins play for keeps.'

'We don't know the local bikie gang is even involved Max. I'll catch up with you and Jack at lunch.'

'Got it.' Max opened the door and exited, Jenny grabbed her jacket and joined him. Liz watched the door close and hoped deep down that the Harlequins weren't involved because if they were, things were going to get ugly.

****

Jack rubbed his wrists as he walked into the grey dull daylight outside the courthouse. Liz's lawyer had been magic to watch. She must have spent half the night preparing for the bail hearing.

'You look like shit,' Max offered as he passed a coffee to his ex-partner, meeting him halfway up the granite stairs.

'I don't feel much better mate. Didn't sleep a wink last night, not that it was advisable. Holding wasn't exactly full of my best buddies.'

'Anyone touch you?' Max puffed out his chest as though he was ready to knock heads.

'No mate. Seems even they believed I might be involved in organised crime, so weren't game enough to touch me just in case. Maybe dad's reputation preceded me.' Jack took a long, slow sip of his cappuccino not even concerned it was in a disposable cup, not his reusable mug. Every muscle in his body seemed to relax as he swallowed.

'Jenny's keeping her head down, but her ears open. Liz is, well,' Max shrugged and grinned, 'being Liz. She's got contacts, as you can guess, even in the bikie world. Any idea why the Bikie Task Force raided you?'

'I've got a few ideas. Nothing concrete yet.'

'Yet! You've been hamstrung mate. You might have to sit this one out on the bench.'

'Not happening. I'll keep a low profile because I don't want to stuff up my bail conditions but I'm going to nail the bastard who set me up.' Jack drank the rest of his coffee as they got into Max's company car. The car still smelt like new and Jack marvelled that Max hadn't sullied the ashtray on the silver sports model Mazda yet.

'How did the bail hearing play out? You've pissed off a few big wigs lately. With Judge McDonald being busted and the federal MP having to roll over on him in that missing girl case, and sniffing out your dad's operation when Liz's friend was killed, you've upset a few top dogs lately. Two corrupt Judges in a matter of months, I hope you found a good one for your hearing?'

'It wasn't easy, but I'm pretty lucky both Liz and you believed I wasn't involved. Thanks for that by the way.'

'Never doubted you. Not for a second. Rickard and Johnnie, they're doing a good job looking into your old man's case?'

'My dad keeps a pretty tight ship Max. You of all people should know that. I've not been able to find a shred of evidence connecting him with anything illegal, so why would anyone try to kill him? He wasn't a liability for anyone! I doubt either detective has found a reason any more than I have.'

'Well, you've been set up, so someone thought you knew something. Maybe it's related to another case? We'll keep digging.' Max started the car and pulled out of Victoria Square away from the courthouse heading to Glenelg and Jack's seaside apartment. 'Guessing you want a shower and to get your car before we meet Liz.'

'You guessed it. I'm not sure I want Liz poking around in this Max. It smells really dirty and she's nearly got herself killed twice now.'

'I don't think you have a choice mate, but I warned her to be extra careful on this one. She knows the bikie scene Jack. I think she'll wait before rushing in if she finds anything.'

'I hope so. I don't know what I found, but someone is trying to mess up my reputation. Not sure if it's anything to do with dad's poisoning. It could just be, like you said, I've upset a few top dogs lately.'

3

Liz checked her phone. She read the message again and wondered if she was being careful enough. She put the phone back in the waterproof pouch strapped to her arm and continued jogging along the concrete pathway that followed the River Torrens through the beautiful parklands.

The air was frigid and the lightweight long-sleeved top she was wearing wasn't keeping her warm at all. She needed to keep running to prevent cooling down or cramping. Keeping her eyes open, she carefully stayed in plain sight, not stopping until she saw Nick.

He was sitting on a concrete bench along the path, and gave her a subtle nod as she jogged past. Liz recalled how his grey beard had once been ginger and his now smoky grey eyes had been a bright, crystal blue. She took the left-hand pathway up toward the Adelaide Festival Theatre just as drizzle began to fall.

She stopped under the cover outside the smaller playhouse often called the Space Theatre and began a series of stretches. There were few people around at this time of day. Most were at work and it was too early for the matinee sessions at the theatre. A big sign in the darkened window showed an art exhibition was due to begin this coming weekend, while a cabaret style show was currently featuring.

Liz jumped at the sound of a deep male voice even-though she had been expecting company.

'Looking good as always Lillian.' Nick used her escort name. She painstakingly kept her real name and life to herself and she'd managed to separate her two lives for over twenty years.

'Thanks Nick. You're looking better now. Last time I saw you I thought you weren't long for this world.'

'I wasn't, but thanks to you, I'm clean.'

Liz studied the man in front of her closely. Slimmer than he used to be, but not as emaciated as he was when Liz pulled him off the streets back in two thousand and one. A former badge member of the Renegades outlaw motorcycle gang, he'd taken to drink and drugs too much after his daughter was killed in a gang shooting gone wrong.

'Don't thank me Nick. You made it back on your own. No one but you can make that type of recovery.'

Nick smiled. 'I wouldn't normally stick my head back into club business, but I owe you one.' Liz waited. She was taking a risk even letting Nick know she knew Jack, but it was one she had to take. She hoped Nick really had cut ties with his bikie roots. It was a hard road out for most.

'I appreciate it. Jack helped me find Becca's killer. It's important to me to help him out. I owe him a favour.'

Nick's eyebrows rose. 'That's all it is?'

Liz grinned. 'You sound like Connie. Once a whore, always a whore Nick. Max, a corrupt cop yes, but a clean-cut private school boy like Jack...' She left the rest unsaid. She didn't want anyone, not even Connie knowing how much she really thought about Jack. Heck, she hadn't even decided herself how much he meant to her.

The drizzle intensified over the parklands and Liz moved closer to the building to avoid the wind that whipped around the large, concrete and glass structure. Nick moved around the outside of the windows, peering inside as he spoke.

'Word is his dad, you know about his dad, right?' Nick looked sideways and Liz nodded. 'Old Judge Cunningham was trying to, how do you say it, extricate himself from some dealings. Harlequins' dealings.'

'Go On.' Liz continued to stretch and run on the spot as Nick wandered around the windows, stopping to pretend to read a program. Other than the remnants of a tattoo on his neck, he looked respectable in his long coat and clean blue jeans.

'Well some of his partners weren't very happy to let him go.'

'A hit?'

'Not sanctioned by badge members, that's for sure.'

'A novice or an associate?'

'Maybe. The Harlequins would have worked it out with the old man without trying to kill him. Judges aren't easy to keep on the payroll. They get too skittish, too often.'

'Thanks Nick. We're even. I won't ask you to stick your neck out again.' Liz did one final stretch as the drizzle eased. It hardly ever really rained in Adelaide, it was just drizzly and windy all winter.

'Not by a long shot Lillian. You need anything, you let me know.' Nick walked away through the undercover area heading toward the centre carpark and North Terrace. Liz jogged in the opposite direction, back down toward the Torrens River to finish her run. Her mind was racing as she pondered what Bruce was really into.

The fountain that sat in the river sprayed mist into the sky, increasing the moisture in the air. Liz pulled her cap down over her eyes, trying to keep her frizzy hair under control, while attempting to ensure no one recognised her. The walkway went up through Elder Park and under the City Bridge, but Liz opted for a more public route. She smiled as she thought how Max and Jack would be happy to know she was keeping an eye on her surroundings, but years on the street had taught her how to be careful.

She jogged up the hill past the heritage gazebo that hosted many events on the parklands. Stopping at the top of the pathway on King William Road, she caught her breath. Checking her watch, she decided it was time to head home for a shower before lunch with Jack and Max. She stopped at the crossing next to Parliament House and waited for the lights to change.

The cold wind howled down North Terrace, sending icy barbs through her already wet clothing. It was a less than ideal way to talk to Nick, but she had to be sure no one would see or overhear them. Nick had fought back from a rough patch in his life and Liz had no intention of getting him in any trouble with his old gang or their arch rivals, The Harlequins.

The warm air flooded from the apartment building as Liz entered the foyer and jogged over to the elevator. She waited, stomping her feet on the spot until the doors opened. Visions of warm coffee and gluten free donuts filled her mind as she made it to her apartment.

She had one more thing to do before meeting Jack, other than a warm shower. She needed to ask Scott, her IT guru, if he could do a little background check on Rickard and Johnnie. There was something bothering her about who could have framed Jack and brought the Bikie Task Force down on him. Sure, there was a really good chance it was The Harlequins, but they had to have someone tip them off that Jack was closing in.

****

'Jenny. Dead homeless guy in the South Parklands. Looks like it might not be natural causes. Meet Doc Holbrook on scene.' The Chief stood in the doorway, waiting for Jenny to collect her coat. She'd only just arrived, the office was quiet. Rickard and Johnnie were out, only two other detectives were sitting at their desks, finishing up from the night shift.

Jenny wondered why the Chief had caught the case and not one of the two detectives still on duty. She decided now was not the time to question her senior. He didn't look in the mood as his eyes scanned the desks lined up in pairs facing one another in the office area.

'Seen Beavis and Butthead yet today?' Jenny tried not to laugh.

'No sir. Just arrived myself. Looks like they're running late.' Jenny collected her bag and holstered her weapon before squeezing past the Chief toward the elevators. She pressed the button and then watched as the Detective Chief Inspector of CIB stomped down the hallway towards the Operations Room.

He was a rare sight in the Major Crimes Division. Sure, they'd all been dragged into his office from time to time. Everyone knew the man, but why would he be delegating a homeless man's death case to her?

The elevator dinged and the two previously mentioned detectives pushed past her as the Chief entered the corridor from Ops. Jenny hopped in and pressed the carpark level as the chief called out, 'Where the hell have you two been?'

A few moments later, Jenny reached the carpark and saw the police officer in charge of vehicles.

'Hi Sam. Can I grab a car? Jack's not in so I can't use his.' The officer looked at Jenny a moment then nodded. She wondered if everyone already knew about Jack's arrest, but guessed they likely did. Gossip travelled faster around the police headquarters than a school canteen.

'Sure Detective. Just fill out this form.' Jenny took the clipboard from the officer and ticked boxes, filled in her name, badge number and signed.

'I'll have it back by five.'

'Okay.' Sam handed her the keys and took the clipboard. 'Is Jack okay?'

Jenny shrugged. 'I haven't seen him yet. Max was picking him up this morning and taking him home.'

'You tell him we know it's a load of cock and bull. Okay?'

Jenny smiled. 'He'll be happy to hear that. Thanks Sam.' She tossed the keys in her hand a few times as she walked to the vehicle, pressing the unlock button to be sure which car she'd been issued.

A few minutes later she was driving down South Terrace. She spotted the Coroner's vehicle and two ambulances on the grass by the Adelaide Pavilion tram stop. Pulling her car into the driveway that led to the Pavilion, she couldn't help but wonder what a strange spot it had been for a homeless person. They hung out around Light Square and in the South Parklands, usually near the oval. The Pavilion was a fancy function centre and security moved the homeless on exceptionally quickly. They weren't exactly good for business.

'Jen.' Penny opened the back of her forensic unit van as Jenny got out of her vehicle. 'Heard about Jack. What a load of crap.'

'Sure is.'

'Max's looking into it I'm guessing?' Penny pulled out two heavy bags and Jenny shut the van doors for her as they both moved into the crime scene.

'Can't say too much Pen. You know how it can be with this type of investigation.' Penny nodded and pursed her lips to exaggerate that she'd say no more.

'What have we got?' Jenny asked as she ducked under a tree branch bordering the tram line from the parklands.

Penny carried the two heavy bags over the rough terrain easily. She was the same height as Jenny, but with broader shoulders and was used to lugging the equipment around, through awkward locations.

'No idea. Just got here myself. The Doc called me in.'

'Okay, so not a standard homeless death then?'

'Guessing not.' The two women stopped as they reached the tram line. Pieces of body were strewn all over the tracks, the tram was stationary, empty of all passengers.

'Holy shit.' Jenny looked up and down the tracks, speechless as Penny put her bags down and opened one, getting straight down to business.

'Quite the mess hey.' Doctor Fred Holbrook looked like he'd just been dragged out of bed. His grey hair was thick and wiry, like he'd put his finger in a light socket. The dark rings under his eyes made him appear older than he was, but he always had them, whether he was fresh out of bed or dog tired.

'Sure is. Where do you want me to start?' Penny surveyed the scene. 'I think I might need a few more bags? One body bag isn't going to cut it.'

The doc laughed. 'Not by a long shot. Start with the hands and head. We need to identify this guy if we can. Fingerprints, then teeth. Let's go ladies, we have quite a few hours ahead of us.'

Jenny saw a group of passengers waiting outside a bus on Peacock Road. She called a uniformed officer over. 'Can you get the names and addresses of all these witnesses? Make sure you check drivers' licences okay?' The officer nodded. 'Then get them on the bus and out of here.'

'Will do Detective.'

Jenny turned and joined Penny as she made her way toward the victim's head, which had rolled clear of the tracks and lodged in the drainage ditch on the far side. 'Do you think he was alive when the tram hit him?' Penny shrugged at Jenny's question.

'Preliminary exam says no.' The Doc moved forward to explain his findings. 'The torso is over there with one arm and one leg still attached.' He pointed toward the front of the tram. 'Rigor mortis has either not set in or passed, but the lividity says he's been dead at least six hours. Besides, there's little or no blood on the scene. It likely congealed before the tram hit him.' The Doc swept his hand in a circle and Jenny followed his arm.

He was right, body parts were everywhere but there was very little blood. 'He died elsewhere maybe?' she speculated.

'Not necessarily. I haven't determined cause of death yet. He might have died of a heart attack last night, collapsed on the tracks and then got hit by the tram this morning.'

Jenny pulled her mobile out and opened her internet browser. A few seconds and a few pages later she looked up at Penny and Doctor Holbrook. 'Not likely. The first tram comes through here just after five a.m. on a Tuesday. He's been laid on the tracks before this latest tram. I'll see you at autopsy later today for an update.' Jenny rushed off to find the driver, hoping he was still on scene.

She spotted him giving a statement to a uniformed officer. He was a greyish white colour and looked uncomfortable sitting on the bench at the tram stop. Jenny approached, the officer looked up as she showed her badge and acknowledged her with a nod.

'Sorry to interrupt. I'm Detective Williams. You must be in a state but I have a few questions.' The driver was in his early sixties, a little overweight, his moustache all grey and his head bald. The man nodded and the officer waited patiently. 'What time did your tram leave Glenelg?'

The man looked at the officer who indicated he should answer the detective's question. 'Six Forty.'

'So you're what, the fourth, fifth run through here for the morning?'

'More like tenth or eleventh. We run every thirty minutes from just before five in the morning.'

'Thanks for your time.' Jenny nodded and turned to walk away.

'Did I kill that man?' The driver might easily have vomited.

'We can't say for sure, but the pathologist believes he was already dead when your tram hit him.'

'Oh thank god.'

'You better get him to see one of the paramedics before he goes,' she said to the officer and moved away. The man looked like he could have a heart attack or die of shock at any minute. She couldn't blame him. It would barely have been sunrise when he came through at just after seven a.m. He wouldn't have even seen the body on the tracks.

Jenny walked back toward her car but stopped when a piece of the victim's upper arm caught her eye. It was covered in tattoos. She pulled a glove out of her back pocket and slipped it on her right hand.

'Penny,' she moved toward the forensic scientist, the upper arm in her hand, 'can you take some photos of this and email them to me as soon as you can?'

'Sure.' Penny slipped the severed hand she'd been holding into an evidence bag and wrote the date and case number on the outside with her permanent marker. Placing it in a plastic crate, she then turned to take the heavily inked arm from Jenny. 'Something look familiar?'

Jenny shrugged. 'It might be nothing, but it could be a link to another case I'm working on.' She was thinking about Jack's false arrest and a bikie connection. The tattoo was just nudging at her memory, but loads of people had them. They were the new body piercing replacement. She had friends who had spent more than a year's worth of mortgage payments on 'body art'.

But this tattoo looked rough, maybe jailhouse or military kind of rough. The edges were blurred, the colours basic, the design ominous. A skull with two automatic rifles crossed through the eyes was hardly fashionable body art. She quickly took a single snap on her mobile so she'd have something to ponder while she waited for all the photos from Penny.

'Thanks Penny. I've got to run. See you later for an update.'

4

'Your regular Signorina?' Nino pulled out a chair as Liz took her regular seat. The North Terrace café was her favourite. A genuine Italian café feel with old Italian décor, not a white subway tile or fake succulent in sight.

'My regular coffee thanks Nino. I might order something different to eat today. I had a really light breakfast and I'm pretty hungry.'

'Good to hear. You could do with some meat on those bones.' Nino smiled, his Italian accent rolling off his tongue. The Italians like their ladies soft and cuddly. Liz returned his friendly smile.

'I have friends joining me, so I'll order when they get here.' Nino nodded and headed to the counter to start on Liz's coffee. The door opened and the wind swept in, fluttering the chequered tablecloths and causing paper napkins to take flight.

Jack entered, followed by Max. Both held thick long coats up around their necks with one hand, but let them go as Max pushed the front door shut.

'It's foul out there.' Max took a seat next to Liz, Jack sat opposite. Liz saw how tired he looked but said nothing.

'Jenny will be here soon. She got caught up with an early case this morning. Ready for coffee?' Liz waved to Nino who was already bringing her coffee over.

'I could use a smoke and a beer, but coffee will have to do,' Max sighed.

'It's lunch time. You can have a beer with your meal if you want Max, on me. But I thought you gave up smoking?' Liz frowned, a slightly disappointed look in her eyes.

Max shook his head. 'No beer, I need to keep my wits on this one. Besides, I'm trying to cut back and yes, I gave up smoking. I only said I could use one, didn't say I'd have one.'

Liz's eyebrows shot up, she looked at Jack to offer his opinion on where the real Max was hiding, but there were no wise cracks today.

'We'll sort this out Jack,' she offered confidently. 'I've got some news already and I think Jenny might too.'

Jack looked up as the door opened once more and Jenny hurried in. Her hair was tied back in a long pony tail but it whipped wildly all the same.

Nino put the coffee down and waited for the orders.

'Jack, you having your usual?' Liz asked. He shrugged and she frowned. 'Regular cappuccino two sugars for Jack, caramel latte for Jenny here.' Jenny nodded the affirmative. 'What are you having Max?'

'The largest mug you have, double shot cappuccino, thanks.' Nino smiled and placed menus on the table in front of everyone as Jenny put her coat over her chair.

Jack didn't pick his up, and Liz worried over his attitude. He was usually such a go-get-em kind of guy. But he looked beaten before he'd even started to fight.

'Let's order then we can get down to business.' A murmur of agreement ensued from everyone except Jack.

'Veal Scaloppini, that's got my name all over it.' Max tossed the menu down like it was a done deal.

'Hmmmm.' Jenny pursed her lips as she focused on the options. 'The Sicilian spaghetti with sardines looks good.'

'Okay, I'm having the basil chicken breast and veg. What about you Jack?'

'You pick something,' Jack offered with no real enthusiasm.

'Don't be a wuss.' Max punched him gently on the arm. 'We'll get this sorted out but you can't hide in a hole now. You were obviously getting somewhere. We'll compare notes and see what you found. Now pick something to eat yourself.' Liz could see his ex-partner didn't like Jack's mood. It was not like him at all. They'd never seen Jack look down, solemn yes, but never depressed.

'Max is right.' Liz's tone was getting frustrated. 'We can't fix this without your help so stop feeling sorry for yourself. You can't piss off Judges and MP's and expect to walk away unscathed.' Liz pointed her finger at the detective with the last few words. His eyes met hers and the corners of his mouth turned up.

'You saved two girls and you solved Becca's murder. This is nothing but trumped-up charges and you know we'll get to the bottom of it.' Liz saw his smile and knew she was getting through.

'Yeah. You have the three best detectives in town on the case with you.' Jenny offered as her sickly-sweet coffee arrived and Nino took their orders.

'Okay. What did you find out Liz?' Jack asked as Nino returned to the kitchen to put their order in.

'I spoke with a former Renegades member.'

'You what?' The old Jack was back. Liz put her hand up.

'We go way back. He's trustworthy and we met somewhere out of sight.'

'You went somewhere out of sight with a known member of the Renegades?' Jack twisted his coffee cup around with agitation.

'*Former* member and *friend* and we were in a public place, just not a busy one. I told you, I'm not new to being covert Jack. Staying under the radar is what I do, remember?'

Jenny put her hands up between them. 'Time-out you two. Jack, let her finish.'

Jack looked at Max for reinforcement, but he just shrugged and the detective sighed. 'Okay, sorry! Go on.' He took a long slow drink of his coffee, his expression showing how much he needed it.

'Anyway, word is Jack's dad's poisoning was a hit, but unsanctioned. Possibly a club novice, but definitely not a full badge member. Either way, the Harlequins weren't happy.'

'So the Harlequins didn't do it?' Jack leant forward, his interest piqued.

'Well, not exactly. My friend said your dad was involved with the Harlequins in some way. Maybe he'd turned over a few cases for them, who knows, but apparently, he wanted out. The Harlequins weren't about to let him go, but they didn't want him dead either, they wouldn't have wanted the attention.'

'No, they wouldn't. Outlaw gangs usually bribe, blackmail or threaten officials into playing along.' Jack frowned as he thought about his dad.

'How is your dad anyway?' Jenny asked.

'He's out of hospital. It's like he's had a stroke. His vision has deteriorated, while not totally blind, he can only see shapes and colours now. The doctors say long-term brain damage, not unlike a stroke victim, is likely. Memory loss, difficulty concentrating, that kind of thing.'

'How's your mum coping?' Max tapped his friend on the shoulder in sympathy.

'She's going okay, all things considered. Dad won't be helping out any outlaw bikie gangs again anytime soon though.'

'So what did you find out that would have marked you for a frame up?' Max drained the last of his coffee and pushed his mug toward the middle of the table. 'You must have found something?'

'The forensic team told me the poison was methanol and likely administered orally in alcohol. Dad collapsed in court, during his late afternoon session, so estimates are he drank the methanol up to seventy-two hours beforehand, depending on how much he'd ingested.'

'And they couldn't say how much he'd had?' Liz nodded her thanks as Nino placed her food in front of her, then the others. No one touched their meals and no one spoke until Nino left the table.

'It took them a while to work out it was methanol poisoning, not a stroke or heart attack, so best guess is he had the alcohol at dinner the night before or later.'

'Where did he have dinner?'

'At home, with mum, but then he went out for a meeting. I tracked down his movements to a bar in town. I hadn't worked out which employee served him yet. I'd called in and spoken to the manager, that's as far as I had got.'

'So you think he was poisoned in the bar?' Max looked at Liz, an unasked question in his eyes.

'Had to be.'

'Well.' Max stopped speaking and frowned when Liz tapped his leg with her foot. They both knew that the bar didn't have to be the only place, but Liz had no intention of jumping to any conclusions just yet. Max took the hint and recovered quickly. 'You must have raised someone's attention. We'll start with the bar. I'll make a visit tonight. What was it called?'

'I'm going with you.' Jack picked up his knife and fork, looking like his appetite had returned.

'I don't think that's a good idea mate. Planting drugs in your place was only the beginning. Just a warning. If they think you're still digging, they'll likely get heavy-handed.' Max cut into his veal and looked at Liz to back him up.

'That's only if my stitch-up is connected. I'm not just sitting here on my hands. I'm suspended pending further investigations, but I'm not going to stand by and get shafted.'

'Go visit your dad. See if he can shed any light on why a non-badge member from an outlaw bikie gang would try and kill him and what he's done to piss off the Harlequins,' Liz suggested before she started on her own meal.

'I don't think that's a good idea.' Jack stopped eating, his expression uncomfortable.

'Jack, he's a crooked bastard, but he's the only family you've got other than your mum,' Jenny offered before slurping up a mouthful of spaghetti.

'She's right. Go talk to him. If he's as sick as you say, you might not get another chance.' Liz thought about her mum as she spoke, feeling like a hypocrite for having not seen her for thirty years. Jack looked to be trying to read her mind as he watched her eyes, then returned to his food.

'Well, doesn't anyone want to know what *I* found today?' Jenny twirled her fork in her pasta.

'Okay, what you got?' Max spoke with his mouth full, at least some things never change Liz thought.

'I found a victim on the tram tracks today. I know you're eating Liz but he was in pieces, lots of them.'

'Oooh.' Liz screwed up her nose.

'Anyway, I found his upper arm, well part of it and there was a tattoo that I thought was strange.'

'Was he killed by the tram?' Jack finished his meal in record time and placed his cutlery down neatly. Liz smiled at his private school boy etiquette.

Jenny continued to twirl her pasta. 'No, sorry, rookie mistake I should start at the beginning. The Chief caught the case, super weird that was.' Jack and Max exchanged looks as Jenny continued. 'Anyway, he came down personally to tell me to investigate and when I got there, Doc told me the guy died before the tram hit him. He thought maybe heart attack, but that didn't fit with the tram timetable.'

Jenny filled her mouth with pasta and Max sighed. 'And?'

Jenny put up a finger. 'I'm hungry, give me a sec,' she spoke from behind her hand, covering her full mouth, then carried on chewing then swallowed, but started to load her fork once more. 'Someone must have put the body on the tracks between tram runs, before sunrise. The tram that hit him was like the tenth tram for the day.'

'So before dawn, the killer dumps the body on the tracks hoping to mess up any evidence.' Jack looked sceptical. 'Why not put a pair of cement shoes on him and dump him in the bay?'

'Why indeed?' Max left his knife and fork scattered on his plate, then dumped his napkin on top.

'Okay, so back to the dead guy.' Liz directed the conversation.

'Yeah.' Jenny pulled her phone out. 'Penny is sending me case photos, but I snapped this one of the tattoo that caught my eye. We are still waiting on an ID, running prints, dental records, you know the drill.' Max and Jack nodded.

Jenny handed the phone to Jack, who looked at the photo and frowned. 'A pretty rough job.'

'I know. I'm thinking a jail tattoo.'

'So your body could have form?' Jack passed the phone to Max who faced the screen so Liz could see too.

'Well it's not a Renegades' or a Harlequins' tattoo,' Liz offered and Jack looked at her, waiting for further explanation. None was offered.

'That would be too easy. I know a few guys who might recognise it. Can you text me a copy?' Max asked and Jenny nodded.

'Are you thinking this dead body is connected to our novice or associate bikie?' Jack directed his question to Jenny, who finished texting the photo to Max and put her phone back in her pocket.

'It could be a coincidence, but if Liz's source is right, and a wannabe bikie tried to kill Bruce, then this might be our guy. The Harlequins could have knocked him off for stepping out.'

'It's only street talk, but he's usually got his ear to the ground. He has to know how to stay clear of any trouble since he left the Renegades.' Liz watched Max stand to leave, Jack joined him.

'Let's hope we can bring someone in who knows something. Ring me if you need an arrest. I don't want Beavis and Butthead on the case,' Jenny added as she stood to put her coat on and join the boys.

Jack looked at her and she grinned. 'That's what the Chief called Rickard and Johnnie. I can't think of them any other way now.' Jack and Max laughed.

5

Jack knocked on the front door of his family home. The feeling in his stomach told him this was a bad idea, but Liz was right, if his dad didn't make it, he'd never forgive himself. Besides, this was business. He heard the sound of footsteps on the timber floors before his mum opened the door.

'Jack! Oh, what a surprise. Come in.' His mum opened the door wide and Jack wandered down the old, expansive federation hallway to the open living area within the modern extension at the rear of the original homestead.

'Is dad up for a visitor?' His mum closed the door, holding the handle with her back to Jack for a moment. He turned and noticed her delay. 'Are you okay?' He moved back down the hallway, but his mother turned suddenly, a smile painted on her face.

She was a tall woman, with long hair that she still hadn't let go grey. Jack couldn't remember what her true colour was, it had been blonde, auburn, brunette and every colour in between over the years. She wore fitted slacks and a lightweight sweater. Always the complete hostess. All Jack's school days, he'd never seen her leave her bedroom in the morning without being ready to entertain.

'I'm fine Jack. Your dad isn't great you know. Why do you want to see him?' She moved past him, his mouth open, words refusing to come out. He thought she'd be happy he was there, trying to patch things up with his dad. Was that what he was doing, or was he just trying to nail the old bastard before he died and find out who dumped drugs in his apartment?

'I'm investigating his attempted murder mum, besides, he's sick....' He left the rest unspoken. His mother took a deep breath and turned away, carrying on into the open plan kitchen with the tall, vaulted ceilings and huge floor-to-ceiling windows that flooded the room with light. A section of bi-fold doors led out to a covered courtyard which was full of ferns and palms set around an outdoor pool and spa. His family estate was the epitome of wealth. What else screamed money if not two swimming pools, one indoor, one outdoor, a ballroom with a retracting floor and a large old stone stable converted to house his father's vintage car collection?

'Did you want a cup of something?' her tone suddenly brighter, her smile even more forced.

'I'm good thanks. I just need to ask dad a few questions. Can I see him?'

His mother didn't answer right away. She put the kettle on, got out three cups, with saucers from the overhead glass cabinets, then added tea to the fine-china teapot before looking Jack in the eye. 'He's in the study. Even half dead he can't stay away from his work.'

Jack nodded and walked through the lounge, to the hallway that led to the newer bedrooms and his father's study. He stopped outside the room and composed himself for what he was going to see.

His dad had looked so fragile, so weak in the hospital. The tubes would be gone and his dad would be awake, but Jack knew he wouldn't be the same old arrogant, proud and confident man he was before the poisoning.

He knocked. 'Come in.' The usual *"Come!"* command was gone. Jack opened the door slowly to find his dad, the infamous Judge Bruce Cunningham, propped up in his tall-backed office chair with pillows. A computer sat on his desk and Jack wondered how his almost blind father could see anything.

'Dad. It's Jack.' The man smiled, something Jack had seldom seen.

'I'm almost blind Jack, not deaf. I heard you come in.'

Jack stood at the door, emotions long buried welling up and threatening to spill over. He forced them down with a loud, deep breath. 'I'm here to ask you a few questions.'

'Of course you are.'

'Are you feeling any better?' His father said nothing for a few heartbeats and Jack scanned the room, focusing on the legal volumes and political thriller novels that weighed down the shelves. Once more he felt like a school boy, making idle conversation with his big-wig father.

'That's not what you're really here for Jack. Take a seat. What do you want?' Jack moved to his father's wide antique desk and sat on the edge.

'It is, and it isn't.' Jack peered over the top of the laptop screen, trying to see what his dad was working on. A dictation program sat on the screen, a letter mid-construction still open. 'I'm working, well I *was* working on your case. I felt like I was getting somewhere too.'

'Then?' His dad didn't really seem to need an answer and Jack wondered again if he still, even in his current state, had his fingers in too many dirty mud pies.

'Then the Bikie Gang Task Force found drugs in my apartment. It seems I got too close to finding out who poisoned you.'

'Maybe.' There was a pause. 'Or maybe someone doesn't want you digging further into any of this business. Let it go Jack.'

'You know I can't do that.'

'I've done a lot of unscrupulous things, some you think you know about, some you most certainly don't, but all of it was to protect you.'

Jack looked at his father trying to think of what to say. The big Judge Cunningham wasn't known for being a soft man, but discovering he'd been the leader in an organised crime ring had blown the detective away. Now the revelation that he'd done it for Jack was hard to swallow.

'What did you do to upset the Harlequins dad?'

His father closed his laptop and sighed as he readjusted the pillow behind his back. 'I don't think someone planting drugs in your apartment has anything to do with the Harlequins Jack but you're asking the wrong question. If I have upset the Harlequins, it won't be because of anything I've done, it'll be about what I *haven't* done.' A tap came on the door and Jack looked up to see his mum, with a cup of tea in hand. She smiled at his dad.

'I hope I'm not interrupting. Bruce, I made you a cuppa.' She moved to the desk, ready to put the teacup down, but stopped to look Jack in the eye. The teacup hovered on the saucer, not quite making it to the desk as silence loomed between them.

Jack held her gaze a moment longer, then looked at his father, whose expression was unreadable. *Did his mum just stone-wall him?*

'I'll let you know how I go dad.' He stood up and moved to the door. 'I'll be back soon mum. Take care of him.' He left the study and moved quickly to the front door, his mind playing over the look on his mum's face and his father's last words.

6

Liz and Max entered the bar, a seedy little spot hidden near the old stone pubs on Halifax Street. There was a Harley Davidson motorcycle shop on one side and the Majestic Hotel on the other. It screamed bikie bar if ever one did and Liz became aware that she had overdressed.

Her red heels and designer dress didn't fit the neighbourhood, but she didn't feel a leather mini with fishnets and a denim jacket would have sent the right message in this dive either.

Max wore a long trench coat and looked like something out of an eighty's crime drama. Colombo or Kojak came to mind and Liz grinned to herself. Max would make an ideal Kojak, but with hair. She had no doubt he wore his shoulder holster beneath the coat. After being caught out on their last case, he'd renewed his hand-gun licence and permit to carry.

Max nodded toward the bar and Liz led the way. She pulled out a studded leather stool, climbing up the rungs to reach the unnaturally high bar. 'I'll have a scotch on the rocks thanks.' The barmaid raised her eyebrows, highlighting three different coloured eyeshadows which didn't even remotely match her bright red lipstick.

'I'll have a Coopers luv.' Max looked longingly at the younger woman and Liz wondered if it was an act or not. Either way, her features changed and a seductive smile crossed her face.

Max was used to this world and although Liz had been too at one time, she now realised she was out of her comfort zone. Her pool-hall days were far behind her, having been replaced with mega yachts in Monaco and high-society balls.

The tall wooden vintage bar appeared as though it had been lovingly restored. The back wall behind was lined with smoky mirrors and glass shelves, fully stocked with spirits, but the faux marble tables and chrome chairs beyond the bar just looked cheap and nasty.

Two broad shouldered bikies stood at the other end of the bar. The light was dim and it was difficult to make out their club badges, but there was no mistaking the laughing Harlequins on the back of one guy's leather vest.

'Do you work here every night sweetheart?' Max was maximising his charm.

'Wednesday to Sunday most weeks. Why?' She twisted the top off Max's beer and placed it on the counter before collecting a tumbler glass and loading it with ice.

'You're pretty easy on the eye darling, so I'm just checking when I should bother coming back in.' The woman looked from Max to Liz and doubt crossed her face.

'He's not with me. I don't know what the hell he dragged me in here for! He knows I'm chasing high rollers, not... you know.' Liz tipped her head toward the men at the end of the bar. The girl smiled knowingly but said nothing as she poured Liz's shot of scotch.

'Speaking of which, I've heard a few lawyers and big shots come in here on occasion.' Max nodded towards Liz, dressed for a cocktail bar. 'A friend tipped us off this might be the spot for Lillian to score herself a sugar daddy.'

'Honey, no self-respecting businessman comes in here. The type we get in might be rich but it isn't because they are good Samaritans, if you know what I mean.' The barmaid leant over as she put Liz's drink in front of her.

'I'm not sure I can snag a reputable one, I might be past my prime for that. Any one of interest been in lately?

'We get them from time to time, but they don't stay healthy very long if they come in here, not unless they know the boss of course.'

'Stop your gas bagging Narelle.' A bikie with a long salt and pepper beard thumped his empty beer mug on the bar and the barmaid shuffled over.

'What will it be boys?' Narelle pushed her chest out, her ample breasts barely contained by her low-cut, tight fitted button through blouse.

Liz didn't hear what was said, but Narelle's face went pale as she looked from the bearded bikie, back to Liz and Max.

'We've been made and I think she's in trouble.' Max nudged Liz. 'Pay and leave.' Liz was about to open her mouth, but the look on Max's face told her now wasn't the time.

'I think you two are a little lost,' the bikie growled as he walked over and grabbed Liz by the arm, spinning her around on the stool. She used her free hand to pull a hundred-dollar bill from her purse and placed it on the bar calmly.

'Thanks for the drink Narelle.' She shook her arm free as the bikie reached to collect up the hundred. Liz picked it up swiftly. 'It's for the waitress.' She could feel Max's tension even with her back to him, but she wasn't going to be swayed.

'My bar, my money.'

'Oh, this is *your* fine establishment. Okay, this one is for Narelle, she held on to the note and pulled another out of her purse. 'This one is for you. Happy?' The bikie ripped the note from her fingers and scowled.

'Why don't I empty out the whole purse, since you seem to have an ATM in there?'

'Because, you should ask around before making such a terrible mistake.' She pulled out a Foxy Escort Agency card and handed it to him. He looked at it, not really registering what Liz was hinting at. She rolled her eyes.

36

'Oh for crying out loud. Your customers and mine cross paths a lot! Now you might have your own little entourage, sorry, is that too big a word for you, let's try harem of girls, but many of your,' she sniffed like she was snorting cocaine, 'customers don't and they use *mine*. Some of them have connections, if you get me?' Liz was winging it and she really hoped it was working.

The bikie took the card and moved down the bar to show it to his mate. She waved the hundred dollar note in the air so Narelle could see, as she slipped it over the counter onto the work area. The other bikie at the end of the bar looked at the card, then Liz and nodded. Beard boy turned back to Liz, a look on his face that even a mother couldn't love.

'Well get out then and don't come peddling your arse around here again or I'll let the boys deal with you, *our* way.' He threw the card on the bar and Liz caught Narelle's eye. She could only hope the girl got the hint the card was for her.

Max grabbed Liz by the arm, gently, but purposefully and they left. Liz's heart was still racing as they made their way down Halifax Street to where Max had parked the car.

'What the hell was that all about? I thought you were trying to get us both killed!' Max pressed the unlock button on his keys as they approached the car. 'Get in! Hurry up!' He scanned the street before jumping in.

Liz got in and Max locked the doors before starting the car.

'I left my phone number on the first hundred, just in case I got the chance to give it to someone who might want to call me. I couldn't let grey beard have it. You saw the barmaid's face when they spoke to her. She went as white as a ghost.'

'They probably told her they'd knock her head in if she didn't stop gabbing to us.'

'I don't think so. The way Narelle looked at you, not me, made me think it was you they were talking about.'

'Me, why?'

'Because you are Jack's ex-partner and you are Bruce's ex you know what.' Max turned his Mazda onto King William Road heading back to Liz's apartment.

'So you think they worked out why we were there and told Narelle to stop talking?'

'Yep, bet two hundred dollars on it. Now I just hope I don't lose my bet and Narelle calls.'

'She won't call. Even if she knows I'm an ex-cop and has information, bikie chicks never snitch, ever. One girl snitched on the Harlequins once. She bore witness in a case about a motorcycle club president killing her husband right in front of her and her kid. Her testimony sent him away, for life.'

'They do snitch then.' Max parked in front of Liz's apartment building and turned off the engine before turning to Liz.

'No Liz, even though the deal was done, the president was going behind bars for the rest of his life and her testimony had already sealed his conviction, they killed her and her kid. They did it to send a message… Don't snitch on the club. Do so and you die. That chick isn't talking to anyone, anytime, ever.'

7

Jenny took the stairs down to the morgue. It was cold outside, but the temperature dropped even more with every step into the basement. The receptionist who sat at the front counter smiled when Jenny reached her.

'Detective Williams, what can we do for you?' She was unnaturally happy for someone who worked in a freezing cold basement showing people dead bodies all day, but Jenny returned the smile in any case.

'I'm here to see Doc about the victim we picked up yesterday.'

'Yeah, nasty one hey. Sorry about the delay. We'd hoped to be ready for you yesterday afternoon but I think they are still finding pieces this morning.'

'No doubt. Is Doc in?'

'Yes. I'll buzz him for you.' The receptionist barely put the phone down before Doc Holbrook appeared, looking even tireder today than yesterday.

'Wasted your morning detective. I left a message with Major Crimes; you didn't get it?'

'Nope, came here first thing this morning. What's up?'

'It's not your case anymore. I identified the victim yesterday afternoon from prints and dental. He's affiliated, a novice with the Harlequins it seems. The Bikie Task Force has picked it up.'

'No way. They can't do that!'

'I'm afraid they can and they have. They are a federally appointed task force Detective. They take whatever case they deem is linked to bikie gangs or organised crime.'

Jenny sighed and looked past the doctor and the double rubber doors that kept the cold air in the morgue. 'Can I get another look at the body, just to finish up my report?'

'No, sorry.'

'I don't suppose there's any chance I can get that name?'

The doctor shook his head. 'I'm afraid not. You know the rules.'

Jenny huffed, loudly. But she understood the doc was just doing his job. 'I'll speak with the Chief.'

'Give it a go girl but I wouldn't hold my breath if I were you. Anderson is a bulldog.'

'Anderson? Never heard of him.'

'He's a kiwi boy. Big, tats, you'd think he was in one of the gangs he investigates, but he heads up the task force.'

'I'll keep that in mind.' Jenny spun round and headed back up the stairs, her mind tossing up what to do next. She pulled her mobile phone out of her pocket and checked for reception. It was always crappy in the basement. A few steps from the top, she stopped and tapped out a quick message to Jack and Max.

She took the last two steps to the foyer as her phone pinged.

He's a mongrel, not a bull dog. Jack replied.

Any suggestions?

Nope, stay out his way for now.

Connected you think?

Possibly, talk soon.

Jenny looked at the last message from Jack before putting her phone back in her pocket. She started to walk to Headquarters from the Coroner's office. It was a short distance, but it gave her time to ponder who Anderson was and why the Bikie Task Force was muscling in on everything to do with this investigation.

First, they had raided Jack, now they'd taken her murder case. A least she had no doubt the two cases were connected now.

A few minutes later she was in the office, a fresh coffee in hand, collected on the way up from the café out the front.

'Williams, you're late.' The Chief was sitting on the edge of her desk, Beavis and Butthead smirking as she squirmed.

'I was at the morgue Sir.'

'My office in ten.' He got up and strode down the hall toward the elevator, leaving Jenny staring into her coffee cup and the comic duo giggling like school kids.

****

'Close the door.' Jenny stood in the Chief's doorway, her mind racing as she entered and pulled the door closed.

'Have I done something wrong?' Jenny sat down in the chair the Chief pointed at.

'Not yet.'

Helpful, she thought.

'Did you get an ID on yesterday's victim?'

'No Sir. The Coroner didn't get me the details before the Bikie Task Force picked up the case and locked me out.'

'Hmmm. How's Jack going?' The question was from left-field and Jenny stuttered before composing herself.

'He's pretty pissed off to be honest Sir.'

'That's what I like about you Williams.' The Chief's chair squeaked as he leant back.

Jenny frowned, trying to read between the lines. She was only in her first year as a detective. Spending time in the sticks had earned her an early promotion to detective and a quick shift to the city and Major Crimes when the police force came under attack for inequality issues. She never wanted a free ride and sometimes she felt her promotion was politically motivated, but then again, she was a bloody good detective, even Jack said so.

As the boss looked at her now, she wondered if her gravy train was about to explode.

'Thank you, Sir.' There was a moment of silence and Jenny decided to ask the question that had been bothering her since yesterday morning. 'Why hand me the tram body case personally Sir?'

The Chief formed a pyramid with his fingers, rocking back on the springs of his luxury, high back office-chair as he considered her question.

'You want to help your partner?' Jenny nodded. 'Let's just call it a hunch.' He leant forward and picked up a sealed envelope from his desk drawer. He handed it to Jenny, who looked it over and went to open it, but he put his hand up silently and shook his head.

'That will be all Williams.' She looked at the envelope and he nodded. Then she placed it inside her jacket pocket and stood.

'Thank you Sir.' She frowned as she pulled the office door open and walked through. *What just happened?* She touched the outside of her jacket and something in her gut told her she was carrying the crown jewels, but she took a deep breath, thrust her chest out and lifted her head as she headed back downstairs to the Major Crimes office.

The envelope burned a hole in her pocket all morning as she cleared up some paperwork and watched Rickard and Johnnie throw screwed up pieces of paper in their rubbish bin like adolescent basketball players.

She was dying to dig into Anderson and the Task Force and see if she could find out who the victim was, but the police computers were not the right place to attempt it. She pulled out her phone and sent a text to Liz.

We should catch up for lunch

No reply. She pushed her phone aside as Johnnie came over, his fingers lingering on the corner of her desk, walking like a finger puppet and spinning on the spot idly.

'What do you want Johnnie?' She looked up, Rickard was busy on a phone call, his hands waving through the air like the discussion was heated.

'How's Jack?' Jenny looked up, expecting to see a smug look, but Johnnie looked serious.

She shrugged. 'He's not happy of course. Load of bull and everyone in the department knows it.'

'Jack's a good cop,' Johnnie offered.

'You and Rickard any closer to solving his dad's attempted murder?' Jenny decided now was as good a time as any to see where they were at.

'Not really. The Judge was connected, but nothing sticks to him. Other than knowing what the poison was, we can't be sure when he drank it. So we aren't sure where either.'

'So, no suspects?'

'Maybe one or two.' Johnnie looked over his shoulder at Rickard as he slammed the phone down. His partner squinted his way. 'Anyway, just tell Jack to hang in there.' The detective moved away, putting as much space between himself and Jenny as he could.

Jenny's phone pinged and she pushed papers aside to find it.

Sure, my place okay?'

Jenny's thumbs sprang into action.

Done. See you in ten?'

All good.

Jenny put her phone in her pocket, took her wallet out of her handbag and locked it in the bottom drawer, before checking her weapon and putting it back in her holster.

'I'll be back after lunch.' No one seemed to notice, or care, so she shrugged, tapping her coat pocket reflexively to make sure the envelope was still in place.

The temptation to read it on the way to Liz's place was almost overwhelming, but she was a professional, and the Chief didn't want her to open it in public, that was obvious.

8

'You guys better come over.' Liz spoke to Jack on the phone. 'I'll call Max now.'

'Why not? It's not like I'm busy doing anything else.'

Liz didn't have time to deal with his depression right now. He hung up and she phoned Max as Jenny sat across the kitchen counter, a piece of plain paper, with a laser printed message still in her hand.

'Max.'

'Yep.'

'I need you to head over for lunch. Jack's on his way.' Liz knew Max could hear the tension in her voice but he was careful not to say too much. They'd made it a policy to be careful with phone calls, ever since their first case had turned out to have links with organised crime.

Judge Cunningham might not be behind the scenes this time, but plenty of people in high places could order a phone tap without either of them knowing and they knew they'd pissed off plenty of people lately.

'On my way.' The phone went dead and Liz pushed it across her shiny white counter.

'I don't know about you, but I need a drink.' Liz looked at Jenny and waited.

'I'm on duty.' She flicked the piece of paper idly.

'Stuff it. Call in sick for the rest of the day.' Jenny put the paper down on the bench and both women looked at it, not saying another word.

A few moments passed before Jenny looked up and took a slow breath. 'Scotch?'

'Scotch it is.'

The girls were on their second when Jack arrived. The colour was finally coming back to Jenny's cheeks and Liz had finished making lunch.

She opened the door to let Jack in, just as the elevator dinged and Max entered the hallway. 'Come in.'

Both entered and joined Jenny at the counter. 'You've started early.' Max smiled. 'Beer is fine for me Liz.' She rolled her eyes.

'You know where to find it.' Her business partner moved around the kitchen counter, plucking a carrot stick from the cheese and dip platter before opening the fridge and pulling out a beer.

'You want one?' He lifted his unopened beer toward Jack who nodded. He twisted the cap off one and slid it over the bar to Jack, then opened his own and took a long, slow swig.

'What's this all about?' Liz nodded to Jenny who opened the neatly folded piece of paper and handed it to Jack. Max walked around behind his ex-partner and read over his shoulder, whistling aloud at the opening line.

Don't share this with anyone except you know who. Hopefully you've got an ID on the victim by now. I put you on this case because I trust you Williams. Keep digging. Things aren't what they seem.

No one said anything. Max tried to put his beer bottle to his lips, but couldn't even manage that.

'There's only one problem. The Bikie Task Force took over the case this morning and I don't have the ID on the dead guy or the autopsy report. They do, and they aren't sharing.' Jenny reached out and grabbed a slice of cheese and a biscuit from the platter Liz had prepared.

'We saw the tattoo; he's likely the novice Liz was told about. If he acted without approval, why is the Chief on this?

What are we missing?' Jack finally put the letter on the counter and downed a mouthful of beer.

'You're right about the novice. Doc shared that much before refusing to give me anything else. Maybe because the Chief and your dad are close, he's just trying to find out who tried to kill him?' Jenny offered, pushing her scotch aside. She really did need to get back to work and her head was spinning having not had lunch yet.

'Maybe.' Max tapped Jack on the shoulder. 'But I might still be able to ID the dead guy. That tattoo is pretty distinct.'

'Did you get anywhere?' Jack turned around as Max took a seat next to him. Liz pushed hot bowls of soup in front of both men and they looked at her, then the food before digging in.

'Thanks,' they offered in unison.

'Not yet.' Max slurped his soup; it was hot but he was obviously too hungry to wait for it to cool.

'I'm not sure knowing who the guy was is going to help. He wasn't officially acting on the Harlequins' orders. He was a lackey, a wannabe.' Liz put a bowl down in front of Jenny and smiled.

'The Chief said *keep digging*, so the guy's ID might be important, but it won't be the end of it.' Jack dipped his crusty bread in the soup and took a bite. 'This is delicious.' Liz smiled appreciatively.

'What now then?' Jenny stirred her soup and blew on a spoonful.

'We met a barmaid last night at the bar your dad was in. She knows something. I think they recognised Max and told her to keep quiet, but I left my mobile number with her.'

'She won't snitch.' Max repeated his warning from the previous night.

'I wouldn't be so sure.' Liz pulled up a stool and joined everyone eating. The smell of thick chickpea and ham soup wafting through the air.

****

Max and Jenny left as Jack stood and walked to Liz's lounge room, a scotch in hand. Liz joined him, sitting on her sofa and sipping her own drink. 'How *was* your dad?'

'Sick.' Jack took a long sip and swirled his drink, the ice cubes tinkled almost musically in the glass.

'And your mum?'

'I think she likes having him relying on her.'

'Maybe she just wants to keep him close?' Liz stood and put her hand on Jack's arm. He turned to look at her.

'I don't know Liz.' She could sense he was feeling out of control. Jack liked order. He liked his house neat and tidy and all things to fit in the right place. His life was not neat right now and she understood what that felt like.

'It *will be* okay Jack. Honestly it will.' He said nothing, just sipped his scotch, his eyes staring back at the fire that wasn't on. 'Everything seems out of control right now. I know that feeling. When I ran away, I felt like my life was going to fall apart and it did, for quite a while. I went from hell at home to hungry and homeless in the gutter and it took me some time to find my way back, but I did. You will too.'

Jack took a deep breath. 'You're right. My problems are nothing compared to what you probably went through.' He looked at her then, his eyes searching for something. 'How did you do it?'

'One foot in front of the other Jack. We'll clear your name, these cases are linked to your frame-up, I can feel it. When we find the name of the guy who tried to kill your dad, we'll be one step closer.'

'Thanks Liz.'

9

'Scott. I need to know if you can find something for me but we probably should discuss it in person.'

'Okay, at your place?'

'Yep. See you soon.'

Liz hung up and paced her lounge room floor. She checked her phone twice, still no call from the barmaid. It was Thursday night and Narelle would be working, but it was too risky for Liz to return. The bikie owner had made if perfectly clear she wasn't welcome.

Liz moved to the kitchen counter, opened her ever present laptop and clicked on her secure browser. Scott had told her often enough that hacking someone's history was easy. There were pixels and trackable links and all sorts of data-mining software programs and apps that tracked social media and website use. Scott had painstakingly drummed internet security into her, and set her computer up to keep her life private.

Marketers tracking her was relatively harmless, but it was the other sources that could be tracking her that she was really concerned about.

She searched the Renegades and Harlequins outlaw bikie gangs in Adelaide. Since the new Task Force and anti-bikie laws had been introduced, there were no club houses left. The laws were criticised for being overly harsh, not allowing any of the ten bikie gangs that had been declared criminal organisations to meet in groups or wear their colours in public.

Even a gym owned by the Renegades' treasurer had recently been shut down. The club houses had been abandoned and seized by the state government. There were mixed feelings about the laws. Liz was on the fence herself, since she dabbled in a grey area of the legal system with her own agency.

Sure, criminal gangs needed to be put on a leash, but not being able to meet in public with your friends bordered on discrimination and was seen by many as a little extreme. Queensland had introduced the laws and South Australia had followed suit, but only South Australia still maintained such a tight hold on the criminal gang activity. Maybe recent events were the clubs pushing back?

The Renegades and the Harlequins were rival gangs and Liz couldn't help but wonder if Jack's dad's poisoning had been carried out by a rival gang, trying to get the judge out of the mix and make life difficult for another gang. If Bruce was working with the Harlequins, then the Renegades would be top of the list.

She typed in the Judge, the President of the Renegades and the Harlequins and clicked images. Had they ever crossed paths? Bikie gang leaders seldom attended any high-flying functions. It was a long shot, but Liz had to wait up for Scott and she was a long way from being tired enough for bed.

This whole mess had Jack unsettled and that made her agitated too.

The door buzzed and Liz checked the camera on her bench top tablet. Scott's emo face stared back at her through the camera and Liz moved to the door.

'Thanks for coming.' She ushered him inside.

'All this cloak and dagger stuff is getting to be your new norm.' Scott didn't sit. His long skinny legs looked out of proportion with his lean, but less than muscular body. Too many hours sitting behind a computer screen, devoid of sunlight wasn't likely to reward him with pecks and a suntan.

'It's part of the job.'

'Your new job?' A wide grin crossed his face. The black lipstick and eyeliner made him look like something out of a horror movie.

'Yep. Can you hack the police or the coroner's office and find me a report?'

'Straight to the point. Always liked that about you Liz.'

'Can you?' Liz hadn't closed her laptop and Scott looked at the screen.

'I can run facial over this if you want?'

'Oh my god that would save me hours of work.'

'Consider it done.'

'What about the coroner's report?'

'No can do. Sorry. Don't you know anyone in the office who can download a copy of it for you?'

Liz slapped her forehead. 'Of course. Why didn't I think of that?'

'You're welcome.' Scott smiled as he sat down at Liz's computer and started typing. He looked up and saw Liz studying him. 'You don't mind, do you?'

'You can do the facial thing here?'

'Sure. It's an online app I use. I just access it via a VPN for privacy, run the search and it's done.'

'You can see who I'm trying to find?'

'Yep, Judge Cunningham with this guy or this one.' Scott tapped the screen with the picture of both club presidents.

'It's a stab in the dark, but worth a search. Can I get you a drink while you wait?'

'Sure, a beer would be good. Thanks.' Scott tapped keys like a court stenographer and Liz marvelled at his speed. It shouldn't be a surprise considering he lived behind a keyboard.

Liz opened the fridge, took out a beer and twisted the top off. She placed it in a stubbie cooler before handing it to Scott.

He put his hand out to take it without taking his eyes off the screen.

'What sites is it searching?' Liz poured herself a small glass of wine, resisting the urge to fill it to the top. She had company after all.

'Newspapers, social media, charity sites, that type of thing.'

'I don't think the bikies will be attending any charity galas.' Liz put the wine bottle back and took a sip of her drink as she moved around to watch the computer screen. Images flashed and disappeared like cards on a casino table.

An image popped and stopped, a square featuring around the face of the Judge and behind him, in the background was the president of the Harlequins outlaw motorcycle gang.

'Looks like we have a match.' Scott took a swig of his beer and smiled.

'It's not conclusive, but it's something. What event is this taken at?' Liz peered over Scott's shoulder and scrolled the screen to see where the picture was published.

'Vinnie's Toy Run event. Of course.' Liz felt like slapping herself. The only place where you'll ever find a Bikie and a public official at the same event. 'But all the bikie presidents were likely there. We aren't any closer than we were before.'

'Look, let me keep digging. I'll run all known bikie members in the hierarchy. President, Treasurer, Secretary from all known outlaw gangs and see if I can do a more thorough search at home. My computers are faster and can move though these images like lightning.' Scott grinned as Liz considered just how fast that could be. The images had moved too fast to see on her computer.

'Thanks Scott. I appreciate the help.'

'All in a day's work.'

'A night's work for you.' Liz grinned and Scott laughed.

10

Jenny's phone rang and she looked at the caller ID. She swiped the screen as she stepped out of the elevator and entered the Major Crimes office.

'Liz, what's up?'

'I've got a favour to ask.'

'Aha.' Jenny put her coffee and bag down on her desk, Johnnie caught her eye and waved. She returned the gesture with the one finger free on her coffee cup, puzzled by his sudden friendliness.

'Do you think you can ask Penny to access that report we've been chasing?' Jenny realised Liz was being vague, but she knew which report she was talking about.

'Why didn't I think of that?' Jenny tried unsuccessfully not to be annoyed with herself. 'I'll catch up with her for lunch today and see if she can.'

'Great, let me know how you go, and Jenny, be careful.' Liz sounded spooked and Jenny took it seriously. Liz wasn't one to scare easily.

'Don't worry. I will. How's Jack? He looked pretty down when we left yesterday.'

'He's good now. I think anger has taken over his depression. He'll keep fighting.'

'Good to hear. It's weird not working with him and pretty strange working alone.' Jenny looked at Johnnie then, he was still watching her.

'You get used to it. See you soon.' Jenny stared at the blank screen. Liz was a whirlwind sometimes. She put her phone in her pocket and pulled out her desk drawer, placing her bag and gun in and locking it.

She pressed the on button on her desk top computer and waited for the ancient piece of bygone technology to finally come to life. She'd been tempted to bring her own computer in dozens of times but it was against department policy. No doubt her work computer was loaded with spy tech to keep an eye on them all. No wonder they were as slow as dinosaurs.

Johnnie looked like he was about to get up and come over, but stopped as Rickard entered the office. The man walked like an ape, his arms too muscled to sit naturally by his sides, his legs bigger than small tree trunks. His partner was the opposite, tall, lanky and fine boned but Jenny was fairly certain there was a good layer of muscle underneath his loose fitted shirt.

Johnnie looked at Jenny a second and then went back to typing on his keyboard. She couldn't help wondering if he was trying to crack on to her, but the thought slipped away when a tattoo covered officer stormed up to her desk.

Jenny looked up at the New Zealand Maori figure looming over her, attempting to block out all the natural sunlight, of which there was little. It was the middle of winter, but he displayed his traditional tattoos on bare arms, his chest only covered with his police issue bullet-proof vest and a plain white tee shirt.

Strapped around his denim covered leg was an ostentatiously displayed pistol. He crossed his arms over his chest and stood with legs splayed. Jenny sat back in her chair and mirrored his stance, a grin on her face as she took her time to look him up and down.

The officer seemed put off by her response and had the good grace to at least stop pushing his groin forward like it was his best feature.

'Detective Williams?'

'Yes. That's me.' Jenny hadn't uncrossed her arms. She could see Johnnie rise from his chair, but Rickard grabbed him by the arm and shook his head. At least Rickard knew better than to treat her like a damsel in distress.

'You have a copy of evidence that needs to be handed in. Now!'

'I'm sorry but I have no idea who you are or what evidence you are referring to. Maybe you got up on the wrong side of the bed this morning, but there is a certain amount of etiquette that goes into starting a conversation and you've totally missed it.'

Jenny had a pretty good idea who was standing in front of her but the arsehole could at least have the professional courtesy to introduce himself.

'Let's start from the top, shall we?' She saw Johnnie grin. 'I'm Detective Williams from Major Crimes Division, but you already knew that, and you would be?'

'Anderson. Task Force Trinity.' Jenny knew the ridiculous code name the police department had given the Bikie Task Force, but it sounded even more absurd when someone said it aloud. She couldn't help but grin.

'Ah, the Bikie Task Force. I see. You understand how much easier this is with context, right?'

'You took a picture from a crime scene. This case is out of your jurisdiction, so we want it back.'

Jenny unwrapped her crossed arms and stood. She was a tall woman and she liked to use it to her advantage. She moved around the desk, removing the barrier from between herself and Anderson. He didn't budge, but his posture changed. He realised he wasn't intimidating her and it annoyed him, she could tell.

'It was a photo, no big deal. Surely the more eyes you have on this the better, right?'

'Not your problem.'

'I don't understand. You don't want the case solved?' Jenny raised one eyebrow and placed her finger on her lips with exaggerated thoughtfulness.

'It's compartmentalised and you aren't in the loop.' Anderson looked up and down the detective's body as she stood in front of him, challenging him. She smiled as his eyes stopped at all the right places.

She was having too much fun. 'It doesn't make a lot of sense and raises a lot of questions really, but...' she shrugged her shoulders and pulled out her phone. She flicked through her photos and showed the Task Force Detective the photo in questions 'This one right!'

He nodded and watched as she deleted the photo from her gallery. 'We need to take the phone.' He reached for it.

'Not happening. I have other cases I'm working on and unless you have a warrant, you have no authority to take my phone.' She pushed it into her backside pocket. 'Touch it and I'll have you up on sexual harassment charges.'

The detective looked over his shoulder at the other two detectives watching the entire scene unfold. 'Did you share the photo with anyone?'

'I work alone Detective. I'm sure you are aware of what happened to my partner recently.' Her tone said she now held him personally responsible.

Anderson rubbed his chin with his open hand. 'Stay off this case Detective.'

'Or what? You'll find drugs in my apartment too?'

Anderson sneered. It was a penetrating, threatening expression that sent a shiver down her spine but she didn't flinch. 'Be careful Williams.'

'Don't worry Anderson, I will be.'

11

'When you sent me the message to meet for lunch, I thought you meant food?' Penny kicked her sparring partner with a left roundhouse, but Jenny blocked it easily with her right forearm and moved in with a left jab to Penny's heavily padded chest.

'I had a visit today, from Anderson,' Jenny bounced on her toes ready to strike once more, 'the prick forced me to give him that photo I took from the tram crime scene.'

Penny put her gloved hands up, palms forward. 'Okay, well you obviously didn't like him, but I never offered to be your punching bag, so I'm hitting the shower now. You can keep kicking the hell out of that real punching bag over there.' Penny pointed to the corner of the gym as she moved off the training mat toward the bathrooms.

'I'm sorry Pen. You're right. He was just so damned smarmy.'

Penny studied the detective. 'Cute too from what I've heard.' Jenny gave her a foul look.

'Cute definitely doesn't describe detective Anderson. Anyway, let's grab a shower, then kebabs are on me. I have a favour to ask.'

Penny rolled her eyes. 'Give me five minutes to get clean and changed.' Both women entered the long, narrow bathroom. Showers and toilet stalls lined the right-hand side, while basins lined the other.

The gym was a kick-boxing training centre, frequented by many of the city's police force. Jenny nodded to a short haired, stocky woman who didn't bother to cover her nakedness as she left her shower stall.

The woman eyed her up and Jenny gave a curt, but clearly not interested hello as they passed. Penny giggled and the detective gave her a not-too-gentle punch in the arm.

'Oh, shut up.' Penny only laughed harder.

'Does that happen often?'

'Too damned often.'

Jenny collected her bag from a locker and moved into a stall, starting the shower while Penny did the same in the one alongside.

'How's Jack doing?' Penny called over the running water as steam began to drift up toward the ceiling.

'He rolls between depression and outrage. Neither is good.' Jenny pushed the pump on the top of the soap dispenser and lathered up.

'You can't blame him. Any closer to finding out what's going on?'

'That's what my favour is about.' Jenny turned the water off and grabbed a towel from her gym bag. She dried off and quickly dressed, leaving the stall, her hair wrapped in her towel. She stood in front of the mirror at the basin as Penny joined her.

Pulling the towel free, she rubbed her hair, combed it and tied it back in a low ponytail before slinging her gym bag over her shoulder. Leaning back against the side wall, she waited for Penny to finish up.

'How is old grumpy pants going with all this happening?' Penny turned, waving to the door that she was ready to go. Jenny pushed off the wall and waited for the forensic scientist to lead the way.

'Max and Liz are both coping. I never thought I'd see the day that Jack got accused of something like this. It's a set-up and *everyone* knows it, but Jack's still on suspension. If we can't find out who did this, his career is over.'

'Has anyone checked surveillance at Jack's house? Done a forensic check or anything?' Penny opened the gym door and exited into the cold air. The sun had finally broken through the cloud and drizzle, which was rare this time of year, but the bitter southerly wind went right through them.

'I expect the Bikie Task Force would have done that, wouldn't they?' Penny stopped and looked at Jenny, her forehead creased, her mouth open, but no words were coming out. Jenny could tell she wanted to say more but her expression said she was torn over what and how to say it.

'Let's just say they… if a detective were to order me on scene, I might be able to double check.'

'Ah ha.' Jenny nodded. 'Would that need to be a senior detective?'

Penny shook her head. 'Not necessarily.' They started walking back toward the police headquarters, past the forensic building.

'Look Pen. I hate to ask but is there *any* way, *any* chance at all that you can accidentally email me the tram line homicide report?'

'No, I'm sure the task force has my laptop monitored so I can't email it out, but I can access it without an issue, which coincidentally, I have already done.' Jenny smiled and Penny continued. 'The victim is Andrew Brathwaite, bartender at Rosie's Bar on Halifax. He was shot at close range with a double tap to the chest. Ballistics confirmed it was a 38 cal round.'

Jenny switched her bag to the other shoulder as they stopped outside Penny's building. 'Not exactly a bikie gang style killing.'

'Exactly my thoughts.'

'Thanks Penny. I hope I haven't got you into too much trouble.'

'Anything to help Jack out.'

'I'll make that request through official channels. We'll likely have very little time to act before detective Anderson rocks up so be ready first thing Monday morning.'

'On it.' Penny waved and moved through the automatic double doors and into the foyer as Jenny continued toward headquarters.

12

Liz opened the files Scott had emailed her. He assured her they were secure but not to download anything to her own computer.

Five photographs featured Jack's father and the President of the Harlequins. The original one she'd already seen; at the charity toy ride fundraiser gala—another two at Malcolm Light's high-rise development event, which Liz had attended—one outside the casino, snapped by a freelance photographer and put on his website for sale complete with a watermark to obscure it from piracy. The final picture featured just the bikie president, the link revealing it was taken in the Judge's courtroom.

All but the last showed the bikie, Bennie Bridges dressed in formal clothing—something Liz had no idea they did, not in her day anyway. In the final photo, he wore no club colours, but was dressed in a white tee shirt and black leather lace-up vest, a bandana wrapped around his head and his neck and arm tattoos clearly on display.

Liz searched for the case details, wondering why Bennie would have sat in the courtroom that day. She opened a browser window and typed in the date and the Judge's name. The case that popped up made Liz frown. Harlequins' club secretary Kurt Nichols had been released and the case of extortion and fraud dropped due to a lack of evidence. Liz speed read through the article and stopped when she saw the name.

Evidence given by police forensic scientist Fernando Rodriguez had been made inadmissible due to possible chain of evidence issues. The result was Nichols walked. Liz took a deep breath and tapped her fingers on the counter as her mind raced to put the pieces together.

She knew Fernando worked at the police forensic lab with Penny. She knew Max didn't trust him as he'd made that perfectly clear on numerous occasions, but he never gave any indication why.

She wanted to call up her business partner and grill him, but knew that talking on the phone wasn't an option. Instead, she sent him a text to meet her for coffee in the morning. A few seconds later the *thumbs up* emoji appeared.

Liz's mobile rang as she closed her laptop and collected her hot chocolate from the bench. Not her usual night-cap, she'd had a sudden craving for chocolate and a warm drink. The result was pleasant.

'Hello.' Liz answered as she sat down in front of her fire and took a sip of her drink.

'Liz, sorry to bother you. I just thought this was important.'

'What's up Amanda?' Liz never refused to take a call from one her girls, it was policy that whoever was on duty, her or Connie, the girls always knew they could call in. The only confusing thing was that Connie was on tonight.

'I called Connie first, and she said I had to call you straight away.'

'Go on.' Liz sat forward and put her drink down, not bothering to relax back, Amanda's tone had her on edge.

'I don't know if you know but I had a new client tonight, Greg, a referral from one of your regulars.'

'Yes, Connie told me and I keep an eye on everyone's calendar. Are you okay?' Liz felt a chill run down her spine. It had been years since any of her escorts had experienced issues, but there was always a chance.

'Look, I'm fine. He didn't do anything to hurt me or off menu. Nothing like that, but he is weird, seriously weird. The guy wouldn't stop asking me questions about you. Where do you live, do I have your mobile number, why can't he see *you*?'

'Okay, that is off. Don't see him again. I'll report him, cut him off our books.'

'Alright. I'm sorry, I just thought you should know.'

'You did the right thing Amanda. I'm sorry. I must have missed something. I'll check with his referee as soon as I can and I'll compensate you for any blocked-out time you had for him on your calendar. I'll cancel them all now.'

'You don't have to do that. Compensate me I mean. I just didn't want the sicko trying to track you down. He even asked questions in the middle of sex. It was beyond strange.' Liz shivered.

'You did the right thing coming straight to me. Ask your building security to keep an eye out, in case he followed you home.'

'No way. I was extra careful. He didn't follow me.'

'Okay, talk soon, and thanks again Amanda.'

'No worries.' The escort hung up and Liz chewed her bottom lip. Ted would never have sent her a psycho client. No way. She went back to her computer, her hot chocolate forgotten. She pulled up her last work email to Ted and replied to it.

Ted. You recently referred Greg to me. I just need to chat if you have time. Call my number.

She hit *send* and checked her watch. She did a quick calculation. Eleven p.m. in Adelaide made it around eight-thirty a.m. in Houston. She closed her computer and returned to her drink. It was not as hot as she liked it, but it wasn't cold yet either.

Her phone rang again and she collected it from the coffee table. The work phone app was flashing and the caller ID showed a US number. Liz smiled and answered.

'Darlin', how's my little princess doing?' Ted didn't wait to make sure Liz answered. She sighed at the sound of his voice.

'Better now I can hear your voice.' The Texan drawl always sent tingles down to her toes. The man was an oil baron, a billionaire who always had time for his favourite Australian girl. Liz had been his escort for decades and they always caught up whenever he was in town.

'Greg! Sweetcakes I never sent Greg your way. You know I don't really like to share. I'd have you with me permanently if you didn't keep refusing me now wouldn't I?' It wasn't really a question.

'Do you know anyone by the name of Greg Bromley?'

'I do, but he isn't in Australia right now, he's here in Texas, I met with him yesterday and like I said, I don't often refer people to *you* Lillian. Selfish I know, but I like to make sure you have space to fit me in when I'm in Australia.' The way he said 'Australia' sounded funny, but Liz was used to it.

'That is strange. He gave me his name, he arrived before Easter and wanted to see me. I told him I couldn't. He wasn't happy but seemed resigned to an alternative arrangement. My business partner booked him in with one of our girls, after a long delay. It's well past Easter now and he is still here.'

'I'll send you a photo of Greg. Darlin', you in trouble again?' Liz knew Ted was referring to her first case with Jack. He'd given her a warning that she was stepping on some high-flying toes. No doubt she was doing it again.

'You know I like a little adventure Ted.' He laughed, a deep, genuine, right from the depths of his chest kind of laugh.

'Oh how I love your adventurous side. I think I might jump on a plane now and head over. Just the sound of your voice has me as horny as a racoon in spring.'

It was Liz's turn to laugh but she got herself under control quickly. She had work to do, a case to solve. But she knew she would always find time for Ted.

'If you do, you make sure to let me know.'

'Why? Your dance-card all filled up these days darlin'?'

'I'll find you a spot Ted, never doubt it.'

Ted made a kissing sound into the phone and hung up. Liz went to her computer knowing her long term client would be right on the ball with a photo. She finished her hot chocolate as her work email dinged. Opening the file, she took a close look at Mr Greg Bromley. He was around late fifties, smartly dressed, clean shaven with a slightly receding, obviously coloured hairline.

Liz emailed the photo to Amanda and asked her to confirm this was the man she saw tonight. She might already be in bed, she might not. Either way, Liz was done. She pushed her laptop shut, plugged in the charger and headed to the bathroom to brush her teeth and get ready for bed.

13

'Why can't we have a coffee meeting like ordinary people?' Max struggled to suck in air, his cheeks were flushed and he was sweating, even on such a cold and overcast day. 'I'm not exactly *dressed* for the occasion.' He stopped and put his head down, resting his hands on his knees.

'Granted, I should have told you to wear tracksuit pants. You said you wanted to get fit.'

'Well I say a lot of things I don't really mean.'

'How is the hand going?' Liz asked as she jogged on the spot, her hoodie pulled up over her head as the drizzle began to fall.

'It's on the mend. I wish I'd trained more with my left hand though. I've had to spend hours getting used to shooting with it.'

'Why?'

'My trigger finger doesn't have full movement back yet. The doc says it will, but I need to do more physio.'

'How's your aim with the left?' Max shrugged as he stood upright once more, his breathing rate still not back to normal.

'Pretty average, but getting there. I wouldn't guarantee a kill-shot but I can manage a centre mass okay.' Liz began to jog forward again and Max sighed.

'You owe me a full breakfast after this.'

'Keep up, I need to tell you something.' Liz looked over her shoulder and slowed so Max could catch up. 'Narelle hasn't called.'

'Hate to say it, actually, no I don't. Told you so.' Liz scowled as she veered off the river track and up past the Festival

Theatre entrance. The area outside the theatre was commonly called The Plaza and Liz considered the steel geometric sculptures and concrete pavers which would soon be a thing of the past. The theatre was about to get an upgrade, a facelift to bring the outdoor area into a new modern era. Liz couldn't decide if she liked the idea or not.

Stopping, she waited for Max to catch back up, the slope having slowed his progress.

'I was thinking I'd wait outside the bar, in the back alley tonight.'

'Are you nuts?'

'No. Narelle will come out at some stage to empty the bins.'

'You've been watching too many movies.'

'Well maybe she won't. What do you suggest?' Liz had her hands on her hips and her expression was nothing short of frustration.

'I suggest you don't go and see her on your own for one thing, but I just so happen to have run her details Friday.' Liz rolled her eyes. 'She owns an old VW Passat and drives to work.'

'We can tail her?' Max smirked at Liz's wild imagination.

'No, *I'm* going to wait at her vehicle near closing time and ask her if we can talk.'

'That's smart, but *we* are going to do that.'

Max started jogging ahead, but turned to face Liz, jogging backwards, a stupid grin on his face. 'I've been doing this a while. I can manage on my own.' He didn't turn back fast enough and caught his heel on a lifted paver. *Maybe a renovation of the theatre was overdue.*

'What was that you said?' Liz teased as she sprinted off in front of her PI partner, but soon slowed down, she had more to talk to him about. 'I'll go in case she will only talk to a female. You can make sure we are both okay that way.' Liz didn't give Max time to refuse. 'Let's grab a takeaway breakfast from Nino's and then we can find a warm spot to talk.

A few minutes later and the pair was sitting opposite Liz's apartment building in the parklands. There was no sun, but the drizzle had gone and the evergreen trees provided protection from the wind.

'We could go to your place you know.' Max pointed to the building foyer longingly.

'I have a stalker and I want you to find out who he is.'

Max stopped, his coffee hovering in front of his lips. He lowered it. 'Has he tried to hurt you?' The words were carefully measured, the tone suppressed rage.

'No, he called to book with me. I told him I wasn't taking new clients.' Max's face showed his surprise, but he didn't say anything. 'Connie organised a substitute but when she met him, she said he wouldn't stop asking about me. Where I live, what my phone number is.'

'Creepy.'

'Very. Here is picture of the *real* Greg Bromley, a friend of a friend who *didn't* refer him as we were told. My escort confirmed her client wasn't this guy. Must have been an imposter.'

'When did he meet your girl?'

'Friday night at the Hilton, room 1801.'

'Penthouse. Nice. What time?'

'They were there from nine until ten-thirty for sure, that was when the appointment was.

'What, no pre-dinner drinks?'

'No. Contrary to popular belief, not all clients wine and dine the girls before screwing them.'

'Don't need to know.' Max put his fingers in his ears. 'What does your escort look like?'

Liz held out her hand. 'Give me your phone.' He did and she started typing in her website.

'Hey, that's my browsing history there you know.'

'Single ex-cop looks up high class escort. Front page news that one.' Liz navigated to Amanda's page and Max took the phone back, studying the photo too closely before swiping for a screenshot.

'This is business Max. I want to know who the guy is. If he's related to any of our cases and if not, stick a rocket up his arse, got it?'

'Got it. What if he's related to the case?'

'Then we'll track him and see where he takes us.' Max tapped his nose and smiled.

'We'll make a PI out of you yet.'

14

Jenny pulled out her phone and began typing a text message.

Let's catch up for pizza tonight? Nino's or Liz's?

She pushed her phone into her waterproof armband and started jogging. The smell of rain in the air was refreshing. She'd spent years as a constable working in central South Australia where it rarely rained and the land was red, dry dirt and rocks.

Her phone rang and she pressed the answer button, her ear pods picking up the call.

'Hello, Jenny speaking.'

'Nice phone voice. You sure you're a detective?'

'Hi Max. A text in reply would have been okay.'

'You sound puffed.'

'I'm jogging.' Jenny jogged on the spot at the lights on King William Road and waited for the pedestrian walk lights to change.

'Over-rated. I need a hand.'

'Ah ha.' The lights changed and Jenny headed into the parklands, sticking to the pathway so her sneakers wouldn't get wet.

'Well I need your badge to be more accurate. I'd ask Jack but he's benched.'

'What do you need?' Jenny stopped running, lifted her leg up onto the rock wall and stretched her hamstring.

'I need to get some surveillance footage.'

'Funny you should mention that.'

'Really?'

'What footage do you need?' Jenny switched legs and stretched again.

'Hilton hotel Friday night.'

'Hmmm. Not what I need, but you can help me and I'll help you.'

'Okay. When?'

'Pick me up at the west end of Rundle Mall on King William Street in thirty minutes.'

'I can call past your place if you like.'

'No, all good. It's not far. See you there.' Jenny pressed the end call button and turned around to head home. She'd been in Adelaide barely a year now and she knew she needed to get herself her own place, but for now, she was room sharing in an apartment not far from work and just across the road from Rundle Mall.

The streets were quiet mid-afternoon on a Saturday. A few people were lined up outside the Festival Theatre, no doubt checking out a ballet or theatre matinee. The weather wasn't exactly a lazing in the parklands kind of day and although the shops in the mall were still open, Saturday afternoons were only busy around Christmas time.

Jenny jogged down King William Street and entered her apartment building. Her exercise had been cut short, so she took the stairs to the tenth floor. A quick shower, a bite to eat and then she was out on the street, across the road and waiting for Max.

The silver Mazda pulled up a few minutes later. Jenny jumped in and Max zoomed away from the taxi zone he shouldn't have parked in.

'I miss the perks of the job you know. There was a time I would have just pulled out the badge and told the taxi drivers to rack off, but those days are gone.'

Jenny rolled her eyes. Max's reputation for playing in the grey area of law enforcement was obviously well deserved.

'We'll check out the Hilton first. We can do my search afterward.'

Max nodded and pulled across the lanes to the far right. 'What's this other spot you need surveillance on and why when you're off duty?'

'Sharper than the average hey Max.' Jenny made a clicking sound and winked at her boss's ex-partner. 'It's Jack's place. I'm sending a forensic unit, Penny to be more accurate, out first thing Monday. We'll likely only get thirty minutes before the Bikie Task Force pull Penny out, but hopefully we'll find something in that time. I'm checking surrounding surveillance cameras today.'

'Jack will have gone over his unit, you know that, don't you?' Max pulled into the Hilton Hotel underground carpark and wound down his window to accept the parking ticket from the machine. He smiled as he flicked the electric window back up. Jenny had never seen his old car, but she knew it had been on its last legs when Liz bought him a new work vehicle.

'No doubt he did, but did he check surrounding building surveillance? Can he even do that without a badge? Plus, Penny is more likely to find something that isn't obvious. Prints, fibres, anything that might point us to who put the drugs in Jack's unit. She gave me the impression the Task Force didn't request forensics.'

'Maybe the Bikie Task Force had their own team on it. Or better still, if they planted the evidence, they wouldn't have needed forensics to check it out.'

'Look, I think Anderson is a wanker, but I'm not convinced he's a crooked one.'

'He's pretty hot then, is he?' Max grinned as he parked and they got out of the car.

'Nothing to do with how he looks. It's just a gut feeling.'

'Well I wouldn't stake my career on it if I were you.'

Jenny decided to change subjects. Why the hell everyone kept mentioning Anderson's looks was beyond her. The guy was a dickhead, an arrogant arse and anyone would think she was on heat the way they kept going on.

'What are we looking for here?' Jenny shut the car door and waited for Max.

'Liz has a stalker. Posed as a referral from one of her old regulars. Complete bullshit, the guy he claimed to be is still in the US.'

'Really. That happen often?'

'Stalkers? No, not really, but this one has it bad for Liz. Just trying to decide if it's case related or not. Either way, I want to find him and tear him a new one, if you get my drift?'

Jenny grinned. 'You got a photo of him?' The parking lot elevator opened as they arrived and Max pushed ground floor.

'Nope, but I know the girl he was with. We need a snapshot of the guy to run through police records and find out who he is.'

'Won't he have registered at the hotel?'

'Not with his real name luv.' Jenny was tempted to pull Max up on his endearments. Words like *honey, sweetie* and *luv* were all so condescending but she knew he meant no harm. Jack often said he was a bit of a dinosaur. Maybe the world still needed guys like Max. He was all heart but suffered from foot-in-mouth disease when it came to political correctness.

Max asked the receptionist where the security centre was. After a quick flash of Jenny's badge, she pointed down a polished stone hallway leading toward the day spa. Jenny showed her badge to the uniformed guard at the security desk and he nodded and waved for them to follow him.

'Wal, we've got a couple detectives here to check out some footage,' the guard announced as they entered the security room.

A round man about five inches shorter than Jenny turned in his chair. The well-worn chair arm rests spread under the strain of his expanding girth and his middle button threatened to expose his gut.

'Well, well. What have we got here?' The guard tried to stand, the chair coming with him a moment before he pried it back down with both hands.

'We need to get a look at your footage between eight-forty-five p.m. and ten-forty-five p.m. Friday night. Suite 1801 thanks.' Max moved toward the guard who looked from Jenny to him and back to Jenny, a sneer on his lips.

'Do you have a warrant?'

'Do we need one?' Jenny moved forward, her extra height towering over the guard. He rubbed his moustache. 'It's only footage of the hallways, common area. I'm sure the hotel management just wants to cooperate, not hinder a police investigation.'

'I don't know…'

'I guess we could request a warrant.' Jenny looked at Max. 'Then we'd have to cite the fact that the footage we are looking for involved a high-glass prostitute and a suspected stalker.'

'Yeah, I guess we could get that warrant, bring what, five or six uniformed officers down?' Max continued.

'Okay, foyer and the hallway, that's it.'

'Why, what other footage have you got for room 1801?' Max crossed his arms and the guard waved his hand dismissively before leaning over the console and hitting buttons on his keyboard.

'Here, I'm bringing it up now.'

Fifteen minutes later, Max had the photo he needed and they were back in the car on the way to the Bay area.

'Can you run this through facial?'

'Sure. Just take a photo of it with your phone and text it to me.'

'What did you want to catch up tonight for?'

'To let Jack know that Penny will be going through his place and that I have an ID on the tram victim. He's linked to the Harlequins for sure, worked in a bar on Halifax Street, isn't that where Liz and you went the other night?'

'Yep, it was. Sounds like he's probably the guy who tried to kill Jack's old man.'

'But it doesn't explain *who* killed him or why the Task Force pulled me off the case.'

'No, it doesn't.' Max rubbed his chin. 'Then there's who framed Jack.'

'Exactly. Any luck on that tattoo yet?'

'Nothing yet, but you have an ID now. We know the dead guy is likely the guy we've been looking for.'

'Yes, but the tattoo might lead us to who hired him and then killed him. We are fairly sure it wasn't the Harlequins.'

'We still don't know that for sure. Two of my mates still haven't got back to me. Hopefully they can find a link.'

****

Twenty minutes of wandering around the neighbourhood near Jack's apartment gave Max and Jenny four possible cameras with a field of vision of Jack's back door, the only one with street access.

They had managed to access two of them via local security feeds—one from the high-rise apartment building next door and another from a block of shops across the road. Neither had a good view of Jack's back balcony and door. There was still ATM footage and a traffic camera. Both would need a warrant and Jenny was certain they wouldn't get one easily.

'We really should tell Jack we are here and what we are doing.' Max began to go up the stairs to Jack's top floor apartment. 'Besides, it's beer o'clock and I still have a late-night shift trying to hassle the barmaid from Rosie's.'

'But we could destroy evidence Penny will need.'

'Look, Jack is a clean freak and the Task Forced probably finger-printed the place when they raided it. He's likely cleaned it from top to bottom by now.'

'Okay. I'll send Liz a text to meet us here for the pizza then.'

'Let's make sure Jack's home first.'

Max led the way up the stairs and along the balcony to the back door. He was just about to knock when he realised it was ajar. Max reached for his gun, on the wrong side and switched hands. Jenny saw him, but she wasn't carrying. Her weapon was locked in her apartment.

She tapped him on the shoulder and patted her empty chest where her holster would usually be. He nodded, understanding she couldn't back him up. They switched places, Jenny taking the lead. Keeping low she pushed the door open and rolled into the room aiming for the space behind where she knew the kitchen counter was. Max moved in behind her, pistol raised, scanning the living area.

'Jack?' Max called out as the curtains on the patio doors blew into the room. Max nodded toward the front balcony as Jenny pulled a knife from the kitchen block, rolling it in her hand to hold the blade downward.

'Jack!' Max called again, still no answer. He circled to the left, pointing for Jenny to take the inside wall. It was the safest spot for her, with an obscured view of the sliding glass doors, and the curtains still drawn across it, she was out of the line of sight or any gun fire.

Jenny moved slowly down the right-hand side toward the open door. The curtains billowed with the strong south westerly wind and Jenny thought she saw a shape, climbing over the railing. She darted forward, Max meeting her at the door. She pulled the slider fully open and Max moved through, gun raised just as hands disappeared from the railing.

'What the!' Max ran forward, extending his weapon over the railing to the ground below. A heavy-set figure limped quickly toward the foreshore, past the adjacent apartment building.

'He's getting away!' Max flew with uncharacteristic speed through the living room, out the back door, down the stairs and into the parking lot, before making a beeline for the alley leading to the beach.

Jenny struggled to keep up, but Max had the weapon so she wasn't exactly itching to get too close. Max stood on the edge of the retaining wall that held the building allotment back from storm-surge damage. He scanned the sparse crowd but couldn't find his target.

'Where the hell is Jack?'

As if on cue, the detective walked up the concrete stairs from the beach below. He wore a full-length wetsuit, a long-board under one arm, his wet and sandy hair was stuck to his scalp.

'What's up?'

'Oh,' Max was huffing now, 'nothing much, just chasing down an intruder in your place! That's all.'

'What?' He looked at Jenny who still held the kitchen knife in her hand.

'He jumped off the front balcony.'

Jack was jogging up the alley way, Jenny and Max trailing behind. He laid his board down next to the stairs and headed up, pulling off his wetsuit as he made it to the door. He examined the broken latch, the chip out of the door and the open door on the patio side.

'Shit!'

Jenny pulled out her phone and dialled. 'I was going to call forensics in on Monday to check the Bikie Task Force hadn't missed any evidence left by whoever tried to frame you, but they can come early now.'

'Hang up.' Jack ordered and Jenny immediately did as she was told.

'Why?'

'Because I want to make sure whoever was here didn't dump another load of smack in my place first.'

'Good point.' Max moved inside. 'You can't come in dripping wet, you could stuff up evidence. I'll grab a towel and a change of clothes while I check.'

'*Then* we call forensics.' Jenny looked at Jack for confirmation.

'Yep.'

15

'He jumped off the balcony? You must have really surprised him.' Liz took a bite of pizza, then got up to refill her wine. 'Anyone need a top up?'

'Beer for me.' Max spoke through his mouthful of pizza. Liz looked at Jack and Jenny who both nodded.

'He must have known where Jack was and about how long he'd be.' Jenny took the beer Liz returned with, and opened the screw-top lid. Liz placed two more beers on the table and returned to get her wine.

'So, whoever it was knows Jack, or is watching him.' Max looked at Jack is if asking him who it could be. Jack shrugged.

'You got my text to make sure Penny is on it, right?' Liz waited for Jenny to confirm with a nod, before putting the wine bottle back in the fridge.

'Always knew Rodriguez was dirty.' Max took another bite of pizza.

'Well mucking up the chain of evidence could have been an accident, but it is strange he still has his job. Either way, I would have put Penny on the case. I trust her.' Jenny took a sip of her beer.

'You're awfully quiet Jack.' Liz watched him carefully as she sat down and picked up her piece of pizza once more.

'Just thinking.'

'Well you know Liz has found herself another stalker.' Max grinned and Jack gaped.

'Why didn't you tell me!' The stare Jack gave Liz dug right through her.

'Because you've been a little busy with your own issues and he isn't a real problem. He just quizzed one of the girls about me, extensively. He claimed to be a friend of a...,' she hesitated before choosing the right word, 'client. But he isn't.'

Jenny sensed the tension rising and changed the subject. 'Anderson made me give over the photo of the tattoo I had yesterday. He even tried to take my phone away, the wanker.'

'I bet that went well for him.' Max grinned and looked to Jack, who had a slight twist of his lip at the thought.

'I shoved it into my butt pocket and I told him if he tried to take it without a warrant I'd have him up on sexual harassment charges.'

'Good on you,' Liz offered.

'That's a card only you girls can play,' Max replied. 'Can you imagine one of us,' he pointed to Jack and back at his chest, 'trying to claim sexual harassment?' Jack warned his former partner with his eyes, but the big oaf wasn't known for his diplomacy. 'We'd be laughed out of the office.'

Liz pursed her lips, but to Jack's surprise managed to bite her tongue. 'Forensics will be in my place most of the night.' He quickly changed the subject. 'You sure you checked everywhere Max? The last thing I need is another charge against me.'

'I checked everywhere mate. Dunny, drainpipes, speakers, roof space. Short of having a sniffer dog, I checked for anything that might cause you issues. Guns, dope, even porn. Didn't find anything.' Jack sighed in relief.

'You won't be able to get back in tonight, so you can stay here.' Max's eyebrows rose toward Liz and a stupid grin crossed his face. 'I've got a spare room,' she hurriedly added as Jenny put her hand over her mouth to stifle a giggle.

'I appreciate the offer, but I'm good.'

'What are you going to do, sleep in your bloody car? That's just stupid. What do you need? A promise that I won't molest you?' Liz pushed her chair back and nearly tripped over it as she left the dining table, stomping toward the kitchen with her empty plate in hand.

Max and Jenny shook their heads at Jack who took a slow, deep breath. 'The spare room sounds good. Sorry. I know I'm being an arse at the moment. It's only that I'm really pissed off about all this crap. Who the hell was in my apartment and why?'

Liz stayed in the kitchen clearing up, obviously annoyed. Everyone knew she never cleaned up when guests were still in her home.

'I'd like to know why Rickard and Johnnie are dragging their feet? They are two steps behind us all the way on Jack's dad's case. We know Andrew Braithwaite is the barman who likely poisoned Bruce. We know he's the dead guy, killed to look like it was a bikie hit. We've been told it wasn't sanctioned by the Harlequins and evidence suggests that's correct. But whenever I speak with either of the detectives, they say they've got diddly squat.' Jenny reached for the last piece of pizza before asking. 'Anyone want this?' Both the guys shook their heads, smiling at her appetite.

'Maybe they have nothing, maybe they just aren't sharing. Either way, we need to know how or who tipped off the Task Force about drugs at Jack's place. Now there's been a break-in at his place, Jenny might be able to convince Anderson to get that ATM and traffic cam footage you were talking about. Then we might see who planted the drugs at Jack's place.' Liz had composed herself and returned to offer her opinion as the conversation got interesting.

'And how am I going to do that?' Jenny licked her fingers and reached for a napkin.

'Oh, I don't know. I'm sure you can use that charm of yours.' Liz tilted her head to the side. 'You *know*, you're an attractive woman and I'm guessing you can get a little information relatively easily with a little charm.'

'See, sexual harassment only works one way.' Max pointed his finger between the two women and even Jack laughed.

'No, he and I haven't seen eye to eye. Besides, he's not my type.'

'This is business Jenny. Everyone is your type when you want something. Play along. Maybe he likes a little feisty competition. Make it work for you.' Liz looked at the boys for confirmation.

'Treat it as an undercover assignment,' Jack suggested.

'You want me to seduce another cop to get information?'

'Exactly. Find his triggers, use them to your advantage,' Liz prompted.

'Liz is the expert at that.' Max surveyed the faces who all stared him down. 'What? It was a compliment.' The silence remained. 'Wasn't it?'

'Alright. I'll see what I can find out.' Jenny gave up arguing.

'Maybe see what Johnnie and Rickard are up to as well.' Jack took a long drink of his beer.

'Johnnie *has* been acting weird, almost friendly, and Rickard has been more aloof than usual.' Jenny frowned. 'The Chief did tell *me* to keep digging, not Johnnie and Rickard.'

'Maybe I should tail them?' Max offered.

'We've got Narelle to see tonight,' Liz reminded him.

'I know that. On Monday, I'll follow Beavis and Butthead around and see exactly how hard they are working to solve Bruce's case.'

'We've got hours to kill before Narelle's shift ends. Cards or Balderdash?'

'Balderdash, what's that?' Jack drained his beer and got up to get another. Liz watched him curiously. She'd never seen him drink so much beer, but at least he was relaxing.

'It's a game where you have a pile of cards with a question on them. There are six categories and you throw dice to decide which category you must play. The dealer picks a card and reads the questions. There is a real answer but everyone who isn't the dealer, makes up a bullshit one and writes it on a card.

The dealer reads out all the answers, including the real one and each player picks which one they think is the real one. You get two points if you guess the right one, one point if someone guesses your fake one or the dealer gets three points if no one guesses the real one.'

'Just watch Liz on this one team. She's good, *really* good at it.' Max warned.

'Well, we're all detectives. I think we should be able to see if she's bluffing.' Jenny looked up as Jack opened the fridge. 'I'll have another. I can walk home from here.'

'Really, where do you live?' Jenny smiled at Max's question.

'Not far from where you picked me up.'

'We'll drop you off on the way to the bar if you want to hang around that long.' Liz agreed to Max's offer with a nod.

'Sounds good.'

'You want a top-up Max?' The PI looked at his watch to gauge how long before he had to drive, then looked at Jack who was standing with the fridge door open.

'Sure.'

****

Liz sat in her living room, a glass of scotch in her hand, the firelight flickered, casting shadows across Jack's face as he sat across from her on the sofa.

'She was scared to death Jack. She kept looking over her shoulder like someone was watching her. It was after eleven and the streets were deserted but Narelle was freaked out.'

'What did she tell you?' Jack moved next to Liz, sitting forward with anticipation. He wasn't exactly slurring, but he'd drunk more than Liz had ever seen him consume.

'She said Andy didn't poison your dad. She swore he had no reason to. They were planning on heading north, to the Territory and leaving the Harlequins behind.'

'Maybe he needed money for the trip?' Jack sat back, somehow not convinced with his own speculation.

'I don't think so Jack.' Liz touched his arm gently, resting her hand on his arm as she continued, 'I think he's a red herring.'

'Then why kill him?'

'Why do it so publicly? We were supposed to find him and think it was the bikies, either that or it's a message for the Harlequins.' Jack moved his arm out from under Liz's hand as he took another sip of his scotch, the ice clinked in the glass somehow highlighting the long silence that followed.

'What about the tattoo?'

'Narelle didn't know much about it. All she said was that he didn't like to talk about it.'

'But he hadn't gotten rid of it?'

'No. Max might find out something from his contacts?'

They both leant forward at the same time to put their drinks on the coffee table. As their hands touched, Liz felt her stomach flutter. She smiled, but Jack moved his hand away.

'I'm tired. Where am I sleeping?' Jack stood and Liz joined him, moving closer than she intended, but she couldn't stop herself.

Jack looked down at her, his eyes bleary, his expression unreadable. He moved in closer, brushing a piece of hair behind

Liz's ear. She took a sharp, quick breath and the world stopped for a heartbeat, before he turned toward the hallway.

'Down here?'

'Second door on the left, the first is the bathroom.' Liz took a deep breath and composed herself. 'Everything you need is in the bedroom or bathroom. See you in the morning Jack.' She moved toward the kitchen, collecting the two glasses from the coffee table on the way.

She could feel his eyes on her. He stood at the entrance to the hallway and watched her put the glasses in the dishwasher and fill a clean glass with water. He opened his mouth to say something, but stopped, turned and walked out of sight.

Liz felt the burn in her eyes and grumbled at herself. *Once a whore, always a whore. No amount of fancy clothing or luxury living will change that Liz.*

16

Liz opened her blinds with the remote and dragged herself out of bed. She'd heard Jack start the shower earlier and had been tempted to stay in under the covers in her room, out of sight until he left, but she forced herself to get up.

The previous night played out in her mind over and over. Her sleep had been interrupted all night by dreams, and they weren't the happy or erotic kind. In one she'd come out of the bedroom in nothing but a G-string only to find Jack with a sophisticated lawyer-looking type on his arm. He'd looked at her with pity, like she'd humiliated herself again and turned his attention back to the other woman.

Liz went to the bathroom, had a quick shower and put on the basics, yoga pants, tank, zip up jacket, followed by foundation, blush and lipstick.

'Sorry,' she said as she entered the living area. 'I'm not much of an early bird.' Jack stood in tight fitted track pants and tee, an open hoody over the top.

'All good. Coffee?' He sipped his own.

She nodded. 'You figured out how to work my machine then?'

He smiled. 'Not rocket science.'

'How's your head?' Liz placed her phone on the counter and took the coffee Jack offered.

'Good. Fast metabolism. I burn alcohol off pretty quickly.' That's not all you burn off she thought but said nothing.

'At least one of us has.' She wanted to blame last night on alcohol. Maybe he had refused her because he was a gentleman and they'd both had too much to drink? Yeah right! *Who cares?* she told herself.

'Look, about...' Liz's phone rang as Jack started speaking.

'Sorry, that's work.' She looked at the screen and then Jack's face. He nodded, encouraging her to take it. 'Hello, Foxy Escort Agencies.' Damn, why couldn't it be Connie's day on roster?

'Lillian, Darlin'. Always love the sound of your voice.'

'Ted?'

'Sure is sweetcakes. Just got into town and wondering if we can catch up? I know you're a busy girl, but can you squeeze me in?'

Liz looked up and saw Jack rinse his cup in the sink and move toward the spare room.

'Sure. I just happen to be available tonight.' Her voice was perkier than she felt. Jack returned to the living room, his overnight bag in hand and gave her a quick wave. She tried to read his face, but he didn't look at her long enough.

'What time?' She watched him open the front door and leave without a backward glance. Her stomach did summersaults, but she shook herself back to her call.

'Nine, my usual suite but I'll meet you in the cocktail lounge to save you getting a room key.'

'See you then Ted.'

'Lookin' forward to it Darlin'.'

'Me too.' Her tone said she was, but as she clicked off the call, she couldn't take her eyes from the front door.

* * * * * * * *

Liz wore a short, tightly fitted dress with long, open, flowing sleeves that gave it a cape-like effect. She'd opted for black, matching it with a red ruby necklace and bright red stilettos. As she entered the hotel she realised just how much she'd missed dressing up and her mood lifted.

She entered the bar, swaying her hips, owning her profession, pushing the guilt she'd felt earlier in the day out of her mind. It had no place here. She spotted Ted sitting at a table that overlooked the parklands and the Torrens River. The sun had long set, revealing the lights of North Adelaide, with St Francis Xavier Cathedral shining like a jewel in the crown.

Two gentlemen stood at the bar, one stepped into her path. 'Excuse me, can I buy you a drink?' Liz smiled politely but nodded toward Ted as he met her, taking her hand.

'Sorry fellas but this gal's with me.' The suiter stepped back with a lavish bow and smiled as Ted led Liz to their table.

'You look stunning as always darlin'.' Ted pulled out her chair and waved at the waiter as he returned to his seat. 'I always love this little town of yours.'

'It certainly isn't a Dallas or Houston, that's for sure, but Adelaide has a vibe of its own.' Liz took a sip of the sparkling water Ted already had at the table. 'I didn't realise you were serious about heading back our way so soon.'

'I told you I would. That Greg issue cropped up and I thought I had best be checkin' in on ya. I spoke with the *real* Greg and he had no idea why someone would have used his details. The mystery had me curious.'

'And you just decided to fly half way around the world to investigate it?' The waiter arrived, a white towel draped over his arm, a silver ice bucket with an open bottle of Bollinger in one hand, two champagne flutes in the other.

Liz waited patiently for him to fill the glasses and replace the bottle in the bucket, then put the bucket on the table before she lifted the drink to her lips. The first mouthful tingled her tastebuds and Ted smiled at her expression.

'I had business dealings to tidy up in any case and you know how much I love to visit you. My offer to fly you to the US permanently still stands you know!'

'Ted, it's a lovely offer and I am truly flattered, but I'm an independent gal,' she copied his accent. 'and you wouldn't want me any other way now, would you?' She took another sip of her champagne.

'Ain't that the truth.' Ted saluted with his glass before drinking.

'You have suspicions about who our Greg imposter is?' Liz pushed gently, the investigator in her coming to the fore.

'Not really.' Liz could tell he was holding back, but about what and why? She smiled, deciding to change the subject. Ted could legitimately have business in town, although what a Texan oil mogul needed to visit Adelaide for was a puzzle. As an escort, she'd never really thought about it, but now, with her investigator hat on, she realised South Australia had no oil drilling rigs, not one. The closest was on the New South Wales border, over five-hundred kilometres away.

'How long are you staying for Ted?' Liz took another zip of her drink as the waiter brought over a plate of tapas.

'I took the liberty of ordering a few snacks, unless you would rather go to my room now?' Liz realised he didn't answer her question but he was the client and she was only making small talk.

She looked at the waiter who obviously knew what was going on between them but was skilled enough to keep his mind on the job. 'Tapas would be lovely. I didn't have very much to eat earlier.'

If Ted wanted to go straight to the room, he didn't show it. 'The squid is delicious. I've had it here before,' he said softly as he took the small plate and napkin the waiter had offered and loaded his plate with a chicken wing and two pieces of the squid.

Liz couldn't put her mind at rest. Since working with Jack and Max she'd become in tune with things that she would have let slide just months ago. Ted's visits had never raised her curiosity before. Why now? Was he here just to make sure the fake Greg meant her no harm, or was he worried there was a link to him?

She could feel the champagne going to her head, and decided she should eat something. Besides, tonight was about her getting back into the swing. She'd not seen a client in nearly two weeks, she needed to get her game on.

Liz brushed a stray piece of hair behind her ear and flicked her head as she dropped her stiletto off and slid her foot up along the outside of Ted's leg. His response was immediate. His eyes twinkled as Liz took another, slow sip of her champagne.

'Oh, how I've missed you darlin'.'

Liz lifted her foot higher, sliding to the inside of Ted's leg, stopping just short of his groin.

'I've missed you too.' She moved her foot over his groin with firm pressure. As Ted's body responded, her own joined the party.

In her mind, she saw again how Jack had gently pushed her hair back behind her ear. Forcing the image aside as heat made its way to all the right places, she became aware just how much she'd missed her work and the feeling of power and affirmation it offered her.

The flirting without commitment was liberating. There was no need to wonder about what Ted thought of her past or if she'd revealed too much of herself. Ted wanted one thing and it was easy to cater for. He was a gentleman who liked to pleasure a woman as much as he liked to be satisfied and oh how she needed the release.

'Maybe we should ask the waiter to bring this up to our room afterall?' Ted didn't wait for Liz to respond. He waved for the waiter who came straight over.

'The lady and I will be heading to the penthouse suite. Please have a fresh bottle with some strawberries, whipped cream and dark chocolate brought up as soon as possible. Add it to my tab.' He handed the waiter a hundred-dollar bill. 'This one's for you.'

'I'll bring it up myself right away Sir.' I bet you will Liz thought.

Ted stood, pulled Liz's chair back and held his hand out for her as she stood. The two men who had been standing at the bar were now sitting, watching Liz leave with Ted, his arm wrapped around her waist, his hand firmly on her butt.

The waiter was true to his word. Their order arrived less than a minute after they did. Ted opened the door and the waiter placed the champagne bucket and desert on the small round dining table, accepted yet another tip and left.

'More champagne?' Ted popped the cork on the bottle and poured two glasses. He walked over to Liz who sat at the end of the bed, handing her one glass while taking a sip from his own.

'If I didn't know better I'd think you're trying to get me a little tipsy.' She smiled, the look more sultry than happy.

'No Darlin', I wouldn't want to dull your senses for this evening.' Liz looked past him at the whipped cream and strawberries.

'In that case, let's go straight to the desert, shall we?' Liz stood, walked to the table, put her glass down and unzipped her dress. It fell to the floor, revealing no underwear, just as Ted always liked it. She picked up a strawberry, dipped it in the cream and walked back to Ted who had now taken a seat on the bed.

He skulled his champagne and threw the glass to the side. As Liz straddled him, she placed the strawberry into his mouth, then bit down on it, kissing him firmly. Ted gripped her buttocks and moaned.

He was over sixty, but strong and fit. It took no effort to lift her light frame up and place her on her back on the bed.

'You just wait right there,' he ordered softly before reaching for the whipped cream.

17

'Where's Rickard?' Jenny asked as she put coffee on her desk and looked at Johnnie for an answer.

'Sick.'

'Really?' Jenny couldn't recall the last time Rickard had been sick.

'Jenny, I...' Johnnie was moving toward her desk but stopped as Anderson stormed into the office.

'You!' He moved toward Jenny, who had just put her bag away and drawn her weapon to put into the drawer. She resisted the urge to bring it to bear as Anderson charged across the room toward her.

'Good morning Detective,' she smiled.

'Why wasn't I called when Cunningham's apartment was broken into?' He was looming over her now, his hand pushed firmly against her chest. She grabbed it, twisting it into a reverse position, taking his shoulder with it. He didn't cry out, but he got the message.

'Oh, I don't know. Maybe because I didn't want any of your crew *finding* anything that slipped out of their pockets. She used air quotes as she released his hand. He rubbed his wrist and stepped back slightly, giving her more space.

'You need to be careful Williams. You should have called me.'

'Sorry, I don't exactly have you on speed-dial. Besides, what's it to you? Internal affairs maybe, but the Bikie Task Force, no way. I'm still trying to work out why the hell you were even in on the raid at Jack's place.' Jenny wanted to say more, but held back.

'You've been asking for surveillance footage in the area. You need to stay out of my way on this case Williams!'

'Why? I'm just doing my job. If you were doing yours I wouldn't need to ask for the surveillance videos, would I? In fact, I'm wondering why you haven't got warrants for the ATM across the road from Jack's place and the traffic camera? Why is that Anderson?' Jenny hadn't raised her voice, in fact her tone had become menacingly quiet.

'Not your case.'

'Jack's career is down the toilet if you don't help clear his name. I'm wondering why you wouldn't want to help do that?' Anderson moved in close, so only Jenny could hear him.

'I get it Williams, but this is way above your pay grade.'

Jenny moved even closer, her warm breath made Anderson's hair move as she spoke. 'You want to tell me more, I know you do.'

'I'm watching you Williams.' It wasn't a threat and Jenny wondered exactly what the detective was saying. She questioned him with her eyes, but he just turned and left. Was it all show? She needed to find a way to have a proper conversation with the man, but how?

As he left, she slumped into her seat, the adrenalin making her hands shake as she picked up her coffee and took a long, slow sip.

Johnnie was back behind his computer screen, trying very hard not to make eye contact. What was he going to say? She opened her mouth to speak, but her phone buzzed in her pocket.

'Hello, Detective Williams.'

'It's Max.'

'Hey.' Jenny didn't use his name in case anyone wondered why she was talking with her boss's former partner. There was a reason why the Chief put her on this and she wasn't sure if it was Anderson or someone else that wasn't on the up and up.

'I hate all this cloak and dagger shit. Are B & B in?'

'Just one.'

'Really?' Max sounded shocked. 'So, any point trailing B-One today?'

'Possibly worthwhile.'

'Okay. I'll be down your way in twenty. I think we should catch up too. I've got something to share.'

'Where and when?'

'The coffee shop downstairs.'

'See you there.' Jenny hung up and picked up the office phone. She punched in the extension and waited.

'Crime lab. Penny speaking.'

'Hey Pen. I hate to put the pressure on.'

'I know. I'm running everything through as fast as I can. All I can tell you is I can confirm there were no prints left behind either time.'

'Damn.'

'And Jen, I checked the front door lock.'

'Yeah?'

'It has never been broken into. There isn't a mark on the outside. I even disassembled it on site and checked for internal marks. Nothing.'

'What are you saying? Jack didn't put the drugs in his apartment? Why would he?' Jenny spoke softly, checking to see if Johnnie could hear her.

'I'm not saying that he did, but there is only one reason why the lock on Jack's front door would have absolutely no signs of a break-in, when we know someone broke in.' Penny left the rest unsaid.

'Gotcha.' Jenny hung up and took a long slow breath. As she looked up, she saw Johnnie looking at her strangely. She watched him as she processed what Penny was saying. Someone had Jack's house key. It was the only sensible answer.

Johnnie looked down at his computer screen once more. A thought was going through Jenny's mind. Liz's voice was sounding in her ear. She might have lost her cool with Anderson but Johnnie was another story.

She drank the rest of her coffee and stood, before slowly walking over to Johnnie's desk and sitting on the edge. She smiled sweetly. 'Did you want a coffee Johnnie? I'm just heading to get a top up now.'

He looked at her, then her empty coffee cup and then back into her eyes. 'Ah, guess so.' He frowned. 'Thanks.'

'Just wondering if you've heard from Rickard yet?'

'Nope.'

'So you just know he called in sick?'

'Yep.'

'Did he call you, or the office?'

'Me.'

'How do you have your coffee?' Jenny stood up. 'Do you have a cup?'

Johnnie looked sheepishly. 'No, sorry. Flat white with two sugars. Here,' he reached into his trouser pocket for his wallet, 'let me.'

'No, all good. I'm sure I can shout you a coffee.'

'Ah, thanks.' Johnnie frowned once more as Jenny left the office. She could feel his eyes on her.

A few minutes later she was at the coffee shop, handing her cup to the barista. 'My usual thanks Mike. Plus, can I grab a flat white with two sugars?' The barista smiled and took Jenny's cup.

'I'll have my usual too thanks Mike.'

'Max. Long-time no see. How's it going?'

'Good thanks mate and you?'

'Freezing, but winter can't last forever, right?'

Jenny and Max waited for the coffees to be ready before heading to a low wall that bordered a garden bed in front of the café.

'Rickard called Johnnie to say he was sick. Something feels off Max.'

'I'll keep an eye on Johnnie today. Maybe he'll visit his sick partner.' Max grinned mischievously.

'Penny just told me that Jack's apartment showed no signs of the first break-in.'

'Meaning?'

'The guy Saturday night kicked the door in. There was no doubt it was a break-in, but whoever planted the drugs, had a key Max.'

'Shit.'

'Exactly. Beavis and Butthead just became number one suspects.'

'Okay, but if Rickard or Johnnie have a key, who broke in the other night?'

Jenny sighed. 'I don't know Max. It isn't making a lot of sense.'

'We'll get to the bottom of it, don't worry. I've found out about Braithwaite's tattoo.'

'Have you told the others?'

'Not yet.' Jenny wondered why, but then Max answered her question. 'It's from Desert Storm, an elite special forces team. Braithwaite is ex-military. There is no way a veteran SAS soldier is going to poison anyone.'

'And that's why you haven't told Jack? Isn't poisoning usually a female murder weapon of choice?'

'Exactly.'

'And you really think Jack hasn't already considered that option?'

Max pondered Jenny's words a few seconds before she saw his shoulders visibly sag. 'I nearly said something the day Jack told us the timeline for the poisoning but Andrew Braithwaite looked good for it. He had access, was linked to the bikies who we thought had it in for old Bruce and were tied up with framing Jack.'

'But the cracks are appearing.'

'Exactly. Liz will have told him what Narelle said about her boyfriend. She told us Saturday night that she and Braithwaite were leaving the state. Getting out from under the Harlequins' influence.'

'I think I'll bring Narelle in for questioning.'

'Probably better to question her at her place, keep it on the down low. I'd hate to see the Harlequins retaliate against her. If you bring her down the station, they'll know for sure she's talking.' Max stood up and Jenny joined him.

'Good point, thanks for standing in for Jack.' Max tapped her arm for moral support.

'You're doing fine without him.' She smiled at the encouragement.

'Johnnie was in the office when I left. This is his coffee. No idea what his case load looks like today, so you had better get back to keeping an eye on him.'

'Will do.'

'You going to tell Liz what we know?' Jenny asked as they began to walk back toward headquarters.

'She's the boss and it's her investigation, so yes, I'll tell her and then I'll tell Jack.'

18

The gravel crunched under Jack's tyres as the car pulled around the ugly gargoyle statue that featured in his parent's driveway. It didn't belong there and never had. He'd always hated it, even as a child.

It was nothing more than a status symbol, as though his family wanted to feel like they were from old money, but Australia had no such thing. Most of the early settlers in Adelaide were free settlers, but they certainly weren't there because they were wealthy. Many had endured the two-hundred and fifty plus day voyage to escape English poverty. They were lucky if they had a few coins left after paying for their passage. It made Jack think of modern-day illegal immigrants. The only difference was England had sanctioned the exile of so many poor English citizens.

His family had come into their money generations earlier and it was more luck than anything else. His great, great, whoever, how-ever far back it was, had been granted a lease over a significant holding on the Adelaide plains. The area, like a lot of good farming land was now covered in houses, but back then, his family had built the homestead his parents still lived in now. They made such a lot of money from wheat and sheep that they eventually purchased the land from the government.

Jack shook his mind back to reality. His father was now a wealthy, corrupt judge and his mother a doctor. They say money makes more money and they aren't wrong, whoever "they" were, but Jack always kept the wealth at arm's length. He hated what money did to people.

He stepped out of his old BMW, the same car he had owned since graduating high school. He still recalled how his dad had wanted to take the gift back when Jack joined the Police Force and not gone on to become a lawyer as had been expected.

He took the steps to the porch and knocked, waiting as he heard his mother unlock the door. It puzzled him, she rarely locked it during the day.

'Jack. Good to see you. Come in.' She stepped aside for her son and Jack walked down the hall to the kitchen.

He looked at the counter and saw that his mother had been baking cookies and cake. He pulled up a stool at the Federation styled kitchen counter and sat. The white corbels and fluted panels framed the overhead cupboards above the stove and the off-white handmade tiled splashback rose high behind a copper rangehood.

'How's dad doing?' he asked as his mother joined him.

'About the same. Did you want a tea or coffee?'

'Tea thanks.' His mum pressed the button on the kettle and went back to mixing the chocolate cake with her Kitchenaid blender. Between the sound of it and the kettle, further conversation was difficult, so Jack just sat and studied his mum.

When Liz had told him about what Narelle had said, the hairs on the back of his neck had stood on end. When she had moved close to him and he'd touched her hair, he'd wanted to forget what was going on in the back of his mind, but he couldn't.

The kettle finished boiling and mum made his cup of tea, placing it in front of him on the counter. She reached for another fine bone china cup and saucer from the mirrored back cabinets that were framed with Federation styled glass doors. Jack watched his expression in the mirror and realised his mother didn't need to be a detective to know he was upset.

'The case is going nowhere.' His mum looked up as she lifted the blender and took the cake mix out, pouring it into a pre-greased pan. She passed the bowl to him with the spatula and he smiled.

'Is that what's worrying you?'

Jack took the spatula and wiped it around the edge of the bowl once, loading it with chocolate cake batter. 'Sort of.' He lifted it to his lips and his childhood rushed back to greet him.

His mum waited patiently for him to continue. 'The guy we thought poisoned dad couldn't have.'

'Why?' Jack had spoken with Max on the phone just before he arrived, but he didn't need the call to know what he already knew.

'One, poison isn't usually a bikie gang member's weapon of choice.' His mother watched him a moment then put the cake in the oven and pressed the timer.

'Two,' Jack loaded his spatula again, 'the guy is ex-military SAS. Again, making poisoning unlikely. How long does methanol take to kill someone mum?' Jack casually put the cake mix in his mouth.

She took a deep breath, her hand hovering over a tray of chocolate chip cookies that needed to join the cake in the oven. 'Up to seventy-two hours after ingestion. It depends on the dose.'

'You already knew that, or you checked it up after dad was poisoned?'

His mother put the cookies in the oven and turned to face him. 'I'm a doctor Jack. I just know. Your father asked you to let this investigation go. Why can't you just let it be?'

He pursed his lips and nodded slowly a few times. 'He did, but someone planted drugs in my apartment and I think it's linked to dad's case. I can't just let it lie.' His mother's hand flew to her mouth and he watched her closely.

'Oh my gosh. Jack. That's horrible. Who would do that?' He'd not mentioned the drugs to her yet. It seemed neither had his father or was she just good at hiding it? He thought she looked sincere.

He shrugged. 'I was hoping you might know. Or maybe dad knows?' His tone was flat.

'That's enough.' Jack turned to see his father in an electric wheelchair, stationary in the hallway that led to his study. How the nearly blind old bastard managed to manoeuvre it out of his study was beyond him.

'Dad!' Jack got up from the stool and helped his father the rest of the way down the hallway to the living room. 'You look a little better.'

'Don't give me that shit Jack. Stop grilling your mother. She doesn't know anything about your predicament.'

'Predicament? I guess you could call it that. You seem calm about it all, but then you never did want me on the force.'

There was silence as his dad scowled at him and he returned the expression. His mother wiped her hands on her apron and fidgeted.

'I had nothing to do with it Jack. When you told me the other day, I made some inquiries. That's all.'

'And what do your sources say?'

'I don't have sources, I have friends.'

'Really? Is that Harlequins friends, corrupt Judge friends or maybe someone dirty on the task force kind of friends?'

'Jack!' his mother begged.

'Sorry mum but this is all totally fucked up.'

'Watch your mouth,' his father growled.

'Or what? Someone has already planted evidence to make me look dirty. *Like father, like son*. That's what they said.'

'Oh Jack.' His mother reached across the counter to his hand but he pulled it away.

'I don't know why I came over. Nothing has changed. Still the lies, still the secrets.' Jack pushed his stool back and handed the cake mix bowl back to his mother, almost as an after-thought.

'Jack!' his mother called, but he was already half way down the hall and on his way out of the house.

He jogged down the front steps and got into his car, starting it, then revving the engine as he raced from the estate. His parents were more screwed up than he could ever have imagined. The realisation that Braithwaite couldn't have poisoned his dad left a bitter taste in his mouth. He wanted to call Max, but knew he was busy. He couldn't see Jenny, she was working and didn't need an unauthorised tag-along. Did he want to see Liz?

19

Jenny left Max and took the elevator to the third floor. Johnnie was just heading out the door as she entered. She handed him his coffee.

'Sorry it took a while. Heard from Rickard again?'

'Not since this morning.'

'So you don't know what he's sick with?'

Johnnie shrugged as if to say it doesn't matter and turned to leave.

'Are you still working on the Judge's case?'

'Yep. Just running down a lead now.'

'Really. Anything I can help with?'

'No. I'm good. I'll let you know if it goes anywhere.'

'Really?' Jenny didn't hide her scepticism as she watched Johnnie leave. Taking a sip of her coffee, she pulled out her chair and wriggled her mouse to wake up her computer. She typed her password in and tapped the keys to search the police database for anything on Narelle. Pulling up prior addresses, police records, prior arrests and anything else she thought might be background for the interview. Finally satisfied she had what she needed, she added some notes to her phone before putting it in her jacket pocket.

Opening her drawer, she retrieved her bag and gun. Placing the gun in her holster, she put her jacket on, drank the rest of her coffee and swung her bag over her shoulder. As she left she considered waiting for the elevator but decided to take the stairs.

She collected keys to an unmarked car and walked across the carpark, pressing the unlock button as she approached the line of black Commodores. The indicators on the second from the end flashed. She opened the door and was about to slip into to the driver's seat when someone stepped out from behind the large round pillar near the car.

Anderson walked up and loomed over her, his aftershave wafting in the air.

'Meet me at the gym after your shift. Four okay?' She looked at his eyes, they weren't looking at her, but watching her surroundings, scanning left to right, searching.

'What's going on?' Jenny felt like pushing him out of her personal space, but he was almost shielding her from anyone seeing. The young detective couldn't work out if it was a protective or aggressive stance.

'I'll tell you when we meet. Four.' He moved past her and disappeared back into the unlit part of the carpark. Jenny stood still, frowning into the gloom, the car door still open, the keys in her hand.

'Four it is then.' She spoke to the empty space as she got in her car and started the engine. She rubbed her hands together, trying to get some warmth into them as she turned the heater dial to maximum. Placing her phone in the stand on the dash, she pressed the pairing button and connected her phone to the hands free.

She dialled Jack's number as she drove out of the carpark, idly wondering what to make of Anderson as the call began to ring.

'Jenny.' Jack answered, his usual *"Detective Cunningham"* greeting absent. She felt sick at the idea of him losing his badge.

'Yes Boss. I'm just on my way to question Narelle again, officially, for the record, but Anderson just bailed me up for a meeting.' She didn't say where. The way he cornered her, in the darkened carpark, had her wondering if it was safe to speak on the phone at all. Jack's phone could easily be bugged. 'Actually, thinking about it, we probably shouldn't talk on the phone. Can I meet up with you and Liz after my interview?'

'Sure. I was just thinking about running a few things past Liz. I'll find out where she wants to meet and text you.'

'Okay. Thanks.' Jenny pressed the hang up button and pulled down Agnes Street toward West Terrace, heading for Richmond. A few minutes later, she pulled up outside a three-storey block of flats that looked like it was built in the seventies. The garden was full of weeds and poorly kept native bushes.

Jenny got out of the car and squeezed down the walkway between an overgrown bottlebrush and a grevillea that nearly met in the middle of the path. She stumbled over a raised piece of pavement, nearly falling but regained her balance and took the stairs to the second floor.

She found Narelle's unit at the end of the walkway, just before another flight of stairs heading to the next level. She knocked on the door and waited. The flats had only one entrance and there was no reason to think Narelle would run, so Jenny tapped her foot absentmindedly thinking of Anderson.

A few moments passed and Jenny knocked again. She put her ear to the door, nothing. The detective had a sudden bad feeling, but kept her cool. Moving down to the window that was about six feet from the door, she tried to get a look inside.

There was stuff everywhere, like someone had ransacked the place. 'Shit,' she said aloud and pulled her weapon from her holster as the next-door neighbour opened their door, saw the gun and gaped.

'Narelle, your neighbour,' Jenny asked, the woman nodded, 'have you seen her today?'

'Why, is she in trouble?'

'Not with me, but maybe with someone.'

'What's the gun for then?' The woman was in her late seventies, her grey hair up in rollers, a scarf tied around her head like some old lady from the British television show, Coronation Street. Her feet were covered with fluffy slippers and her cardigan was done up over her sagging braless breasts, the buttons misaligned.

'The gun is just in case. Has Narelle been home today?'

'I don't know. What do you think I am, the local busy body?' Jenny shrugged... that was exactly what she thought, but the woman continued. 'Last I saw her was Sunday lunchtime.'

'Thank you, can you go inside now, just in case?' Jenny thought it unlikely anyone was inside, since questioning the old lady had been loud and taken long enough for anyone to come out if they'd been there. Unless they were waiting inside with a gun?

Jenny tried the door and it opened. As she pushed the door aside, she could see the lock was damaged. She pulled back, considering whether to call for back-up—but what if Narelle was injured? She pushed the door open and stepped back in case someone inside was armed.

There was no noise, no one moving around. She entered, gun raised and knew what Jack would be saying if he could see her. She shouldn't have entered on her own, without uniformed officers and especially not without a bullet-proof vest.

The room was a mess. Jenny cleared the living and kitchen area before moving to the bathroom, then the bedroom. She stopped in the bedroom and turned around to take in the surroundings. Drawers were open, the bed was unmade, there were clothes left in the cupboard, but coat hangers were strewn all over the bed and floor.

She pulled her phone out and dialled.

'Max Fitzpatrick, Fox Investigations.'

'Jenny here Max. I'm at Narelle's. She's done a runner.'

'Really?'

'And that's not all. She left in a hurry. The place is a mess and the front door has been forced.'

'Call in a forensic team, see what they can find. Just have a look around and see if there is anything there to indicate where she might have gone.'

'What if she didn't go willingly?'

'You said she left in a hurry. What makes you say that?'

'There are coat hangers everywhere, drawers are open.'

'She packed in a hurry. Is there a suitcase there?'

'No.'

'So, she either got away, or someone grabbed her on the way out.'

'Exactly.'

'Call it in. I'll catch up with you later.'

'I'm having lunch with Jack and Liz. You going to get away from stalking Johnnie to join us.'

'I lost him at Rickard's.'

'What?'

'He stopped in at his partner's place and went inside. I parked around the corner and headed toward the house to see what I could find. The next minute, Rickard's car pulls out the garage. I had to duck for cover so he didn't see me. Johnnie's car was still parked out front.

'So did he or Rickard go out?'

'No one was left at home so it looks like they both left in Rickard's car.'

'What time was that?'

'About an hour ago.'

'You didn't follow them?'

'No, I was too busy stalking around the house when the car pulled out. By the time I got back in my car, I'd lost them.'

'That's just weird. I'll text you once I know what's happening at lunch then.'

'Okay. I'll make it if I'm finished here in time.'

'Where is here?'

'I'm still at Rickard's waiting for the shitheads to come back.'

20

Max walked into the pub with a broad grin. 'How did you convince him to come here for lunch?' Max nodded to his old partner.

'It was my idea.' Jack offered.

'That makes sense since you're not on duty.' Max saw Jack's face fall. 'At least you can have a drink this time mate.' He tried to cheer him up as Liz and Jenny shook their heads gently.

'What are you having Max? I'll get your order in.' Liz stood with purse in hand.

'I'll get mine.' Jack stood to join her as she turned toward the orders counter.

'Jack. It's okay. I know you're not being paid, I'm good. You can buy me a dinner out sometime, when we get you off these stupid charges.'

There were a few moments of silence, Max looked between Jack and Liz, a frown forming between his thick eyebrows. 'I'll have a steak, medium rare, with chips, no salad.' He offered his order up.

Liz waited for Jack's order. 'I'll come with you to the counter,' Liz huffed. 'You can buy, I just figured you'd need extra hands to carry the drinks.' Liz smiled. 'Good idea. Jenny, have you decided yet?'

'Hmmm. Too much to choose from. But, let's go with chicken pesto pasta.'

'Good choice.' Liz turned and walked to the orders counter. 'You alright Jack?' she asked as they lined up behind two businessmen in almost matching light grey suits.

'It's been a rough few days. I'm okay.'

'You don't look okay.' Liz stepped forward and placed their order. The waitress gave them a plastic number on a tall chrome stand. Liz waved her card over the machine and kept it out as she moved to the bar.

'I went to my parent's place this morning.'

'Oh, how is your dad going?'

'Not great, but that's not the issue. This whole case is making me edgy. Don't worry. I'll be fine.'

'One Pinot Gris and three Coopers Pale Ale thanks.' The barman nodded. 'What's the issue then?' Liz persisted.

'Look, I'm not sure yet. I'm still trying to put all the pieces together, but if Braithwaite didn't try to kill dad, that only leaves...' Jack left the obvious unsaid.

'Well, don't jump to conclusions just yet.' The barman returned with the drinks and Jack took two beers, while Liz took the rest. As they returned to the table, Jenny and Max looked up guiltily.

'What were you two talking about?' Jack put a beer down in front of Max. Liz did the same for Jenny.

'Oh, nothing important.' Jenny shrugged, looked at Max who shrugged just as suspiciously.

'We need to crack this case soon and get this guy back to work.' Max changed the subject and patted Jack hard on the back as he took his seat.

'Well, not sure if it will lead to a break, but Anderson cornered me in the carpark at the station this morning, all spy style, lurking in the shadows type of stuff. Scared the shit out of me when he appeared out of nowhere.'

Liz and Jack exchanged puzzled looks.

'Anyway, he wants to meet with me at four at the gym near work.'

'You be careful Jenny. We have no idea if we can trust him yet.' Jack took a swig of his beer. His face relaxed as it went down.

'Just stay out in the open, you'll be fine,' Liz offered.

'The way he was going on, I don't think he's going to want to talk in the open.'

'You want me to go to the gym and keep an eye on him?' Max suggested. Liz giggled. Jack openly laughed and Jenny sat with her mouth open, trying to think of something kind to say.

'Mate, you don't exactly say gym junkie,' Jack smirked.

'I could be just starting out, you know, on a get fit kick.' Max looked offended. His paunch was reducing and he seemed to have succeeded in quitting smoking but still, he wasn't about to blend in at the gym.

'Look, I usually keep a low profile and Jack can't go. I'll head over and do a few k's on the treadmill.' Liz took a sip of her wine and Jenny nodded.

'That might work.'

'On what planet will that work?' Max crossed his arms over his chest. He hadn't taken a drink of his beer yet. 'Anderson is humungous. He'll eat you for breakfast if he means to play foul.'

'Max, Jenny is pretty capable of looking after herself,' Jack indicated. 'Liz can watch and make sure he doesn't do something stupid. If he does, she can call us.'

Max sighed. He was obviously outvoted. He picked up his beer and slowly drained it, one gulp after another. Finishing, he slammed it onto the table a little harder than intended, causing the table number to topple over.

'I'll wait outside then, within easy reach.' The conversation was over as he got up and returned to the bar for a refill.

'Max already knows this, so I'll catch you two up. I went to Narelle's to see if I could question her, officially for the police records.' Jack and Liz moved aside for the waitress as their orders arrived.

Jenny looked like she might inhale the pasta she'd ordered, but she ignored it to finish the story. 'The place was trashed.'

'She okay?' Liz asked as she began to eat her chicken salad.

'She wasn't there. Goneski. There were coat hangers everywhere, drawers hanging open. She'd packed in a hurry, but someone had broken the door down. Not sure if it was before or after Narelle left.'

'She knows more than she told you.' Jack looked at Liz. 'You said she was balking at shadows Saturday night.'

'She was scared, but we thought that was because the Harlequins saw her talking with an ex-cop, she'd be in trouble.'

'What if she knows more about dad's poisoning?'

'What if she is the poisoner?' Jenny offered just before she put a large fork full of penne pasta in her mouth.

Max returned and sat down. 'What did I miss? I could see the excitement level rise from the bar.'

'Jenny was just catching us up on her visit to Narelle's.' Jack took a swig of beer. 'You think she could be the real perp?' Jack looked relieved at the idea.

'Hmmm.' Max sat down and picked up his steak knife, not replying as he cut a large piece of steak and loaded two french fries on top. The fork hovered in front of his mouth as he spoke. 'Possibly. What's her motive and why did someone kill Braithwaite then?'

'We need to find her.' Liz insisted.

'Did you canvas the neighbours?' Jack was back in detective mode and Liz smiled at his renewed energy. They all knew what he'd been thinking. Hell, they had all though it, but if Narelle was the poisoner, then Jack had someone else to focus on.

'Yep. Crazy old bat next door ran me around in circles, but harmless enough. She hadn't seen Narelle since Sunday lunchtime.'

'Okay, did you ask her about the break-in?'

'She didn't mention it, but I didn't go back after the uniformed officers arrived. They have her statement.'

'I think you need to head back and ask a few more questions. Surely she heard someone kick in Narelle's door?' Jack was back in charge, eventhough he was on the bench officially.

'I've got that meeting with Anderson.'

'Well I don't have a badge so I can't question her.'

'Here, have mine.' Max pulled out his PI badge and handed it to Jack. 'Tell her you are a friend of the family. Her mum lives in McLaren Vale. Tell the old chook that her mum is worried or something.'

'That's lying Max.' Jack protested.

'Yes, but you are suspended already, so who cares?' Jack looked at Liz and she shrugged, then grinned.

'It could work. Maybe the old lady knows more than she's sharing and you can track down Narelle. If she didn't poison your dad, she may know who did and that's why she's on the run.'

Jack took another drink of beer, then a mouthful of his chicken schnitzel and chewed aggressively.

21

Liz jogged into the gym, her cordless earbuds in, listening to *Robert Palmer's Addicted to Love.* Jenny was already sparring on the mat with a guy Liz had never seen. Jenny had described Anderson to her, it wasn't him.

Jenny kicked her tall, lean opponent with a roundhouse kick, that struck his padded side. The air was knocked out of him and his mouthguard flew into the air, saliva spraying in a wake behind it.

Liz found an empty treadmill and stood either side of the belt, slowly bringing it up to speed. She stepped on and began a slow run. Even though she was warmed up after jogging from home, she still wasn't ready for full speed.

Jenny saw her, but didn't make eye contact. Max was outside, in case Liz called for back-up. She could feel butterflies in her stomach. So far, everything she'd done in her new PI role had been questioning and talking about the case. Well, except for the last case when she'd been slapped unconscious and found herself in a damp cellar and then there was the case before that, when someone tried to suffocate her, twice, but this case was different.

Everything had been interesting, but a little routine. A stakeout, a meet-up like this was exciting and Liz had to remind herself it wasn't a game. Jenny was relying on her to be her back-up, just like Jack would have been had he not been suspended.

Jenny bowed to her partner, who moved off the mats. The detective removed the padded helmet and used a towel to wipe her face. Her white tank top was covered in sweat, her hair was tied up in a high pony tail. She wore tights, full length to her ankles and sneakers with ankle socks.

A broad man, with dark skin and tattoos all over his arms moved onto the sparring mat. He wore gloves, a padded helmet and mouth guard, but no other padding. His bare chest made Liz almost skip a beat on her treadmill. She adjusted the speed and kept running. The pace was only about six kilometres an hour, an easy jog for her. The last thing she wanted was to be exhausted if something went wrong.

Jenny didn't smile at the man. His eyes took in her body and the grin on his face said he liked what he saw. Liz studied the detective's body language. Her eyes said no, but her body disagreed.

She couldn't make out the conversation, but then again, she didn't need to. She just needed to make sure Jenny stayed in the open and the Task Force detective didn't try to take her anywhere she didn't want to go.

****

Jenny took her mouthguard out and drank a long slow drink of her cool water as Anderson stepped onto the mat. She saw his gaze move over her body and wondered if he would meet her eyes anytime soon.

'Detective.' Jenny spoke first.

'If you are going to meet me for a date, we should at least be on a first name basis, don't you think? Call me Hemi.'

'This isn't a date Detective. You jumped out of the darkness and commanded I meet you here at four. I don't call that a polite invitation for a date.'

'But you came.'

'I didn't have much choice.'

'I need you to pretend you like me.'

'Why?'

'Because we could be being watched.' He'd moved in close, so only she could hear him speak. His voice was husky and the heat from his body was hard to ignore.

Jenny stepped in even closer, so she could whisper in his ear. 'Cut the shit.' Anderson grinned as Jenny stepped back, her padded fists coming up in front of her face. 'Ready?'

'Born ready.' Anderson moved to the centre of the mat and Jenny bounced toward him on her toes. He was big, but she was agile. She ducked away from his first strike, weaving under his reach and hitting him in the chest, just below his right arm with a short sharp left hook.

His chest was like hitting a fully padded boxing bag. The sudden stop caught her by surprise. He smirked and she screwed up her nose. The wrist-lock she'd used in the office had caught him off-guard. He was ready and waiting this time.

His second attempt was quicker. She knew he was pulling punches, but it struck the padding over her right cheek, spinning her around. He moved in behind her, whispering into her ear. 'You have a mole in your department.'

Jenny lifted her head back, striking him in the jaw, the padded helmet taking the impact, but he moved back, raising his hands to his face, elbows together in case she hit out as she turned. She did, but with her right leg. The jump-kick struck him in the chest again. He stumbled back but didn't fall.

'Not here.' She pulled off her gloves and moved to collect her towel and drink bottle. Anderson moved up behind her, removing his helmet as he moved closer. She stood up from collecting her things. He was right there, a wall of bare chest pushing against her back.

'Why tell me?' She spun around, his face was so close, she could feel his breath on her cheek.

'Because you are digging into Jack's case, which means you don't believe he's dirty.'

'He's not.' She pushed her hands between them to wipe her face with her towel, but Anderson didn't pull back.

'Then he's not the mole and I need to find who is.'

'We can't talk properly here.'

'I'll be in touch. I needed to let you know, you have to be careful Jenny.' He moved back and pulled his gloves off, leaving the mat without another word. She stood still, then shook her head as another opponent stepped up to spar.

'I'm done.' She smiled and left the guy standing in the middle of the mat looking disappointed. She wanted to chase Anderson down, but knew she couldn't.

She headed for the showers. Liz joined her at the entrance.

'What was that all about?'

'I'll grab my bag.' She walked into the change room entrance, where the lockers lined the walls. She pulled the key out of her back-zip pocket and opened her locker, removing her bag and locking it once more.

Liz followed her out of the gym into the foyer that led down the stairs to street level. The green tiles that lined the walls were falling off in spots, exposing white adhesive lines beneath. The girls watched their step carefully in the dimly lit stairwell.

'My place?' Liz asked.

'If you're okay with me taking a shower?'

'For sure.'

'What's going on?' Max met them at the bottom of the stairs as they opened the old aluminium glass door and took the two steps to the curb. 'I saw Anderson leave.'

'He dropped a bombshell and then took off. I'll tell you on the way to Liz's place.'

'Hop in, I'll drive you over.' Max had parked in the *No Parking* zone of the alley off Angas Street.

'I should give you a ticket.'

'Why? I'd just have to add it to the pile in the console.' Max grinned.

'I have to pay for those Max.' Liz grumbled as she opened the passenger's side door.

Max backed out of the alleyway, straight onto the main road. A car honked on the horn, but swerved out and around the shiny silver Mazda. Liz rolled her eyes and Max shrugged as he put the car in gear and took off down the road toward East Terrace.

'What did he say?' Max looked in the rear-view mirror at Jenny.

'He said the department had a mole.'

'No surprises there. I thought *he* was it.'

'Nope. My department, Major Crimes. He thought Jack was it, when they found the drugs. But.'

'Now he's having second thoughts?'

Jenny shrugged. 'Now he's willing to play nice.'

'What else did he say?' Liz turned around to look at Jenny.

'Nothing. He said he would contact me. That too many eyes might be watching.'

'That means he trusts you, but why?'

'He said I was digging so deep into Jack's case, well you were really, but he said he realised we didn't believe he was guilty. I wouldn't be digging if I was dirty and wanted Jack to take the fall, would I?'

'He's sharp.' Jenny wasn't sure if Max was being facetious or not, but decided to believe he wasn't.

'So you don't know when he will contact you next?'

'Nope.'

Max pulled up in front of the Liz's apartment building and the girls got out.

'Thanks Max. See you tomorrow.' He nodded and she shut the car door, waiting for Jenny.

'Thanks for the company. I didn't really want to head back to my apartment and fester over who the mole is and what they've been leaking.'

'Oh, I thought you might want to do some daydreaming about Anderson.'

Jenny scoffed. 'Do you know he told me to call him by his first name, Hemi? And he called me Jenny. Can you believe that?'

'Yes.'

'What?' Jenny stared at Liz as they entered the foyer and walked to the elevator.

'He's got the hots for you honey.'

'No way. He hates me.' Jenny gaped as the elevator doors open and they both got in.

'No. Believe me. I read men and he's totally into you. I think he likes them feisty.' Liz grinned.

'Just like Jack.' The grin disappeared as the doors opened on Liz's floor. 'Oh come on, you know he wants you.'

'Not enough to do anything about it.' Liz opened the door to her apartment and Jenny put her hand on Liz's arm.

'What? Spill.' Liz had visions of Jack pushing the hair behind her ear again and blushed.

'He had his chance and bailed.'

'No way!'

'Yes way, now have your shower.' Liz put her earbuds on the counter and shooed Jenny toward the bathroom when she didn't move.

'You can't just leave me hanging.'

'Shower!' Jenny grinned, but turned to toward the hallway that led to the spare room and bathroom. She stopped, holding the edge of the doorframe and stuck her head back around toward the kitchen and Liz.

'Pour wine. I'll only be a minute and then I want the full story. Every detail.'

22

Jack knocked on the door, watching the police tape on Narelle's door flutter in the breeze as he waited. He heard a voice call out they were coming. Then a few noises, the deadbolt opening and the chain being put in place.

'Yes.' A grey-haired woman peered through the slit in the door.

'I'm.' Jack was so close to saying detective, but stopped himself. 'Max Fitzpatrick. I'm a private investigator. Can we talk about your neighbour?'

'Narelle. Pretty girl, stupid, but pretty.'

'Stupid, why?'

'Who you working for sonny?' The old lady didn't miss a beat.

'Narelle's mother. She lives in McLaren Vale and is worried. She hasn't been able to get Narelle on the phone since yesterday lunch.'

'Really? She never mentioned a mum.'

'I'm not at liberty to explain my client's relationship with her daughter, but she's worried.'

'Narelle stayed here for a few hours. She was here while that police woman was here and the other police searched her home.'

'Did you hear who broke into her apartment?' Jack ignored the fact the woman lied to Jenny. He was supposed to be a PI, not a police detective.

'I heard, but I wasn't sticking my neck out to find out who it was. Narelle knew though and she was scared, really scared. Poor thing. She hid in my bedroom the whole time.'

'Ex-boyfriend maybe?'

'Her boyfriend is dead,' the woman stated flatly. 'I don't think her and the person who broke in were friends, let alone lovers. But the man who broke in had a friend with him.'

'How do you know if you didn't take a look?'

'I wasn't born yesterday. Saw the car parked down there.' The lady pointed through the slit in the door to the carpark below. 'I'm the last apartment, and my loo window looks out over the side there.' She indicated with her head to her left.

'Do you know the model of the car you saw?'

'What's all the interest in who broke in? I thought you were looking for Narelle?'

'I am, but if the people who broke in caught up with her, then I might need to track them down.'

'Oh. Yes. Didn't think of that.' Jack could just see her face as she screwed up her lips and pondered her answer. 'I'm not much good with car models. It was dark blue. Big, with a hatch back door thingy.'

'Four wheeled drive?'

'No idea.'

'Did you take a number plate?'

'Look sonny. I'm an old lady. You're lucky I even got to the loo window before the guy left the apartment and got back in the car.'

'You saw him get back in?'

'Yes, big guy, with a limp but I didn't see anything else.'

'Thank you. You've been very helpful.' The door closed without further comment and Jack stood for a moment before turning to leave. He pulled out his mobile phone and flipped it open, pressing the number '1' speed dial to call Max.

'Mate.' Jack didn't wait for Max to acknowledge his call. 'The guy that broke into Narelle's apartment had a limp. Big guy, with a limp.'

'Shit.' Jack could hear the hands-free background noise.

'And a friend waiting in the car. A big, blue hatchback.'

'Rickard?'

'And Johnnie maybe. 'Why would he be searching Narelle's apartment without a warrant?'

'Maybe he didn't break-in, maybe he was searching *after* a break-in.'

'He didn't call it in. He was there before Williams and he didn't call it in.'

'I didn't see them when they came back this morning. Rickard parked in the garage and Johnnie came out the front door to his car, alone.' Max thought a moment, he needed to catch up with Jack.

'Look mate. I've just left the girls after Jenny's meeting. We need to talk.'

'My place in an hour. I'm still in Richmond and need a shower.'

'Okay, I'll bring the beer.' Max hung up and Jack took the stairs to the carpark two at a time.

****

Jack got out of the shower and changed into jeans and a long-sleeved tee. He walked out to his small kitchen and opened the freezer, pulling out two steaks. He put them on a plate and set the microwave on defrost before pressing start.

The knock didn't surprise him, he'd seen a shadow pass in front of his kitchen window before Max banged hard on the old wooden door.

'It's open.' Max entered, a case of beer on his shoulder.

'Just like old times.' The grin was infectious and Jack couldn't help but join in the merriment.

'You're looking good Max.'

He put the beer on the kitchen bench and patted his stomach. 'I'm working on it. I'm a dad now. Have to be responsible.'

'Jackie is over twenty-five mate, but love the sentiment. How's the quitting smoking going?'

Max stuck his tongue out, a piece of nicotine gum sat on the tip. 'It's going alright. This stuff tastes like shit but it works. Cravings are manageable.'

'Good on you.' Max handed him a beer and put the rest of the carton in the fridge.

'So, what are we going to do?'

'Eat steak.' Jack waved his beer at Max's frown. 'I don't know mate. It isn't making a lot of sense. If Rickard broke into my apartment the second time, he probably wasn't the one who did the first time.'

'Why?'

'Well he broke the door in.'

'Maybe to cover up the first break-in?'

'Maybe.' Jack didn't sound convinced.

'Either way, we've got no real evidence of anything except someone who could be Rickard broke into your apartment, then Narelle's. What we don't know is why.'

'We need to find Narelle.'

'Where would she go? She told us she was going to go to the Territory with Braithwaite, but now he's dead?' Max shrugged, asking the unanswered questions.

'What about her mum in the Vale?'

'They are estranged. I doubt she'd go there, but maybe Liz and I can take a day trip and pay her a visit.' Jack frowned at the idea and Max didn't miss the expression. 'Don't worry mate, we won't do an overnighter, it's not that far.'

The microwave dinged and Jack opened the door to take out the steaks. He took them out of the cling wrap and left them on the plate to finish defrosting while he started to prepare some vegetables.

'What Liz does is up to her Max.' Jack finally answered his friend.

'You got that right mate.' He slapped Jack on the back good-naturedly. 'Liz gave Narelle a card for the agency, the escort agency,' he clarified. 'She might look her up if she needs help.'

'You said the Harlequins recognised you. She won't go to Liz if she thinks Liz knows the cops.'

'Maybe. Depends how scared she is.'

'True.'

'Look, we haven't checked out the Renegades in all of this. Could it be a bikie war after all?'

'Why try to kill my dad?'

'I don't know. Has he done the Renegades any favours?'

'I'll just call in and ask him, eh?' Jack didn't sound impressed.

'I'll ask Liz to do some digging.'

'That's not a good idea. Digging into bikie business could be dangerous.'

'Jack. You're not going to be able to protect her every minute of every day. She's a force of nature mate. She's not your problem.'

'She's everyone's problem Max. She's a loose cannon.'

'She gets results.'

'Two big cases and both resulted in her nearly being killed. That is luck, not results.'

Max shrugged. 'You aren't going to stop her so you have two choices. Have nothing to do with her again. Or come to terms with it.'

'You don't have to feed her opportunities to get into trouble though,' he protested, but Max shrugged.

'She's smart, always has been. She'll join the dots whether we tell her to or not and she'll dig no matter what we say or do.'

23

Jenny put her coffee down and turned her computer on before opening the drawer and placing her bag inside.

She scrolled through her emails and one caught her eye. She opened it and saw the message. It simply said. *Watch!*

She clicked on the attachment, which opened in her movie viewer program. There was no sound, just grainy footage that was difficult to see clearly, but the location was obvious. It was Jack's apartment building and the footage must have come from the ATM across the road.

Jenny squinted, trying to make sense of the scene. It was dark, the balcony lighting was shocking and all she could see was a hooded figure in front of Jack's door.

Moments later, the person entered the apartment and disappeared. Less than two minutes passed and they reappeared, pulled the door shut and left. There was no way of seeing the carpark with the ATM footage and the video was so grainy, she couldn't identify the perpetrator.

She chewed her pen before shaking it between her thumb and forefinger. Rewinding it, she began to view it again, but stopped as Johnnie came over toward her desk. She flicked the video viewer closed and looked up.

'How's Rickard doing?'

Johnnie shrugged and tapped his fingers on the corner of her desk as he stood pensively. She recalled he'd wanted to say something to her the other day, before Anderson barged in.

'What's up Johnnie?'

He looked around to see if anyone was within earshot. There were only two other detectives in the department and neither was in right now.

'I'm not sure yet.'

She frowned. 'Is it related to Jack's dad's case?'

He shrugged again. 'We are both junior detectives.' A silence followed and she nodded to encourage him to carry on. 'I'm not sure if I should say anything.'

The hair on the back of Jenny's neck stood on end. She'd heard from Jack about Rickard and how he'd had someone else in the car. Was that someone else Johnnie? Did he know what his boss was up to?

'Johnnie. What's this about?' She decided to plunge on. 'Is this something to do with Rickard being off work?'

He nodded and she got the impression he was asking her to guess. 'Has he done something you aren't sure is regulation?' Another nod. 'You don't know if you should report it?'

'It's not one thing, it's a few things.' He looked over his shoulder, seeking any prying eyes.

'Make a report Johnnie.'

'I can't.'

He adjusted his position and Jenny noticed a slight wince. 'Look, I know you are digging into our case. It's got Rickard nervous, like he is worried you'll find something.'

'Will I?'

'I've got nothing concrete or I'd make a report. For all I know, Rickard is on the up and up and he just goes about things differently. Old school. You know.'

Jenny frowned. Jack was old school but as by the book as you could be. He didn't even let Liz buy him lunch for fear of bribery allegations. Maybe it was his dad's background but she doubted it. He'd always been like that from what Max had to say.

'You guys have been behind me on this investigation. I've been wondering why. Were you anywhere near Narelle Fergusson's place yesterday?'

Johnnie's eyes went wide. 'He told me he had to question her.'

'Rickard?' She already knew the answer but had to ask.

'Yes.'

'But he was off sick?'

'Injured but he wanted to follow up with her. Said she knew more than she was letting on.'

'Did you go with him to interview her?'

Johnnie shook his head. 'No. He said he'd handle it. I just chauffeured for the day.'

Jenny wondered how much to share with him. He could be covering his arse now he knew she was on the case. Rickard could be the muscle and Johnnie the brains.

'Interesting.'

'What?' Johnnie went slightly pale and she nearly reneged.

'Nothing concrete yet. Like you said. Just if you are worried, make sure you fill out a diary, date it electronically if you can. That way, if anything comes unstuck, you'll at least have some sort of record.'

'You think it will, come unstuck I mean?'

'No idea Johnnie, but like you said, you're a junior detective following orders. If something isn't quite right, you'll have voiced and recorded your concerns.' She looked at his expression and realised he wasn't convinced. 'Rickard isn't a hundred percent by the book, but I'm sure it will be fine.'

She wanted to reassure him and make it look like she was convinced it was all good. The last thing she needed was Johnnie saying anything to Rickard. Johnnie nodded and moved away from her desk. She watched him return to his desk and gingerly lower himself into his seat.

As he took a phone call, Jenny reopened the file she'd been watching. While viewing the second run through, she thought of Liz's IT guy. Opening a new email, she attached the file and added a message to explain to Liz what she thought he might be able to do.

She sent the message to Liz before opening the police database. Typing in Narelle's information, she hit the enter key, launching another search into the woman's priors. Two solicitation cases popped up, a possession charge and some fines for association with the Harlequins. Nothing she hadn't gone over yesterday.

Running known associates, the system brought up her dead boyfriend Andrew Braithwaite and two full badge Harlequins' members. Not a surprise considering she worked in one of their bars.

The solicitation cases went back fourteen years. Narelle would have been barely eighteen. Jenny opened the first case. A photo of a pretty girl with dark blonde hair and crystal blue eyes looked back at the detective. She'd changed a lot since then, Jenny thought. As she flicked the file closed, she frowned and opened it again.

There was something familiar in the young woman's face. She scanned the file and almost whistled when she saw the name of the arresting officer.

'I'm getting coffee Johnnie, do you want one?' She closed all the open windows on her computer and put the password lock in place. Jack had been thorough with her training. It would take a tech to know what file she opened last.

'No thanks. I'm just heading out. New case, dead guy at the Hyatt.'

'Two murders in a week. Adelaide is turning into Sydney,' he chuckled as she collected her wallet from her bag, put her coat on and popped her mobile in the inside pocket. 'I'll take the stairs. See you later.' The last thing she felt like was small talk in the elevator.

She reached the café and ordered her coffee before pulling out her mobile and dialling Jack's number.

'Jenny. What's up?'

'I had an interesting conversation with Johnnie earlier. Not sure about it yet, but I'll let you know if I get more. What I did find was in Narelle's file.'

'I thought you'd been through it already.'

'I had, on the surface. She had priors, but I hadn't really dived into them while Braithwaite was the main suspect, but after the break-in at her flat, I thought I should take a closer look.'

'And?'

'And she has two solicitation arrests. You'll never guess who the arresting officer was.' She smiled at the barista and handed over some cash.

'Not in the mood for guessing games Williams.' The boss tone was in full force, even with a suspension.

'Rickard Barnes.'

'Fuck!'

24

Max cranked the stereo up using the steering wheel buttons and grinned like a kid in a candy store when Liz shook her head. *Cyndi Lauper's, Girls Just Want to Have Fun* blared out of the surround sound system and Max bopped up and down to the tune.

Liz finally couldn't stay stoic any longer and had to start bopping along with him. McLaren Vale was about an hour south of Adelaide and they'd started early. She'd called Narelle's mother to make sure she'd be happy to see them. Happy wasn't the way she would have described the woman's mood, but she was willing to meet with them.

Liz's phone rang and she manually turned the stereo down. Max frowned until he saw her take the call.

'Hey Jack.'

'Hi Liz. Is Max with you?'

'Yep. Do you want me to put you on speaker?'

'Yes thanks.'

Liz pressed the button on her phone to go to speaker, turned up the volume, the radio turned down automatically with the hands free. 'Okay, you're on.'

'Hey mate. Just took a call from Jenny.'

'Okay.'

'She dug into Narelle's file. A few solicitation priors, nothing huge, but the arresting officer was Rickard.'

'No way.' Liz said.

'Yep. Seems they know each other from way back in two-thousand and four.'

'We are heading to meet her mum now. Will see if she knows anything about any history between them.' Max leant over slightly as he spoke toward the hidden speaker.

'Thanks. Did you work with him at all coming up through the ranks?'

'Nah mate. I was based in Adelaide. He spent most of his early years at the Bay.'

'That's what I thought. Jenny also said she sent Liz a video of some footage she had, from outside my place. It's poor quality. Do you think Scott can do anything with it?'

'He'll be asleep, but I'll forward it to him and ask him to follow up first thing tonight.'

'Thanks Liz.'

'Where did the video come from?' Liz asked, looking at Max who shrugged.

'Unknown, but she thinks Anderson.'

'That would make sense. We'll be back after lunch Jack. I'll call you with a progress report.' Liz waited to make sure there was nothing else he needed to share before hanging up.

'If Narelle is involved, is she the stooge or the boss?' Max turned the radio back up a little louder.

'You think we've been played?' Liz put her phone back in her bag.

'No idea. What does the famous Foxy sense say?' Max grinned as Liz rolled her eyes.

'Let's meet the mum first and we'll go from there.'

****

'Thanks for seeing us Ms Fergusson.' Liz took a seat in the sunroom that overlooked the neighbour's vineyard. McLaren Vale was well-known as a wine region, but Liz didn't expect Narelle's mum to have such a lovely home.

'When it comes to Narelle, I have always tried to make time.' Ms Fergusson gestured to a seat in a sunken sunroom before taking a seat herself.

'Lovely home you have here.' Liz was fishing, hoping not to have to ask the question directly. The woman smiled knowingly.

'Yes, this is my place. Now you're wondering why Narelle has been so troubled? You did say on the phone that she *was* in trouble again.'

'Yes, well we think so. We met Narelle after her boyfriend was murdered.' Liz watched Max walk around the room, his hands behind his back like a beat cop, his eyes taking in everything.

'You're police then?'

'No, investigators. It's a long story really, but we've been contacted to help in a related investigation.'

'And what makes you think Narelle is in trouble?' Ms Fergusson sat forward, a look of concern on her face.

'Her home was broken into and she's suddenly disappeared. We think she might know more about her boyfriend's death, or maybe her going missing is unrelated, we aren't sure yet. But we need to speak with her and wondered if she'd come home, to you?'

The woman laughed aloud. 'There is no way Narelle will come to me.' She sat back once more, her emotions teetering so much Liz struggled to read the woman. Did she really care about her daughter?

There was a long silence, as Liz waited for her to continue. She didn't. Instead she watched Max who had left the questioning to Liz, opting to observe the woman's home and surroundings. He stopped at the end of the sunroom and was peering closely at the pictures and family photos on the walls.

'There are no photos of Narelle in here.' Max lifted a family portrait from an old teak sideboard and showed it to Ms Fergusson. Liz could see there was a tall, dark-skinned man and two children with Ms Fergusson, but Narelle was absent. Liz gazed at the other photos and like Max said, the woman's only natural child was missing from them all.

'That's my late partner. He died of cancer a few years ago. We met when I was working in a central Australian aboriginal community as a teacher. He ran the general store there and we just hit it off.'

'That's tough work.' Max put the photo back down on the cabinet.

'I'm tougher than I look.' She held Max with a penetrating gaze. 'The children are twins, adopted from the community. Their father ran away to avoid cultural initiation— he was thirteen and the mother was in no shape to care for them.'

'You brought them here, away from their homelands?' Liz chose the question because she knew cultural connection was important to the Aboriginal community. Australia had experienced the stolen generation and it was now frowned upon to take indigenous children away from their heritage.

'Not straight away. We raised them to high school age in the community. I was the teacher there for over ten years, but there isn't a lot of opportunity for higher education out in the bush, especially not on the homelands. We left with their mother's and the tribal elders' blessing. They still visit often.'

'Where does Narelle fit in all of this?' Liz moved forward on the seat in the sunroom, the conversation coming around to focus on their possible new suspect.

The woman sighed and her eyes became sad. It was the first clear emotion Liz had seen from the woman. 'I was in a bad place when Narelle was little. I blame myself for how she is.'

'And how is that?'

'I raised her on my own. I was studying to be a teacher in her teenage years. She went a little wild.'

'Does she know who her dad is?' Liz continued the questions, Max seemed content to observe once more.

'She does now.' Ms Fergusson looked around the room and smiled a sad smile. 'Everything here I worked hard for. Her father gave me very little. Narelle didn't have any of this growing up.' She waved her hand around the sunroom, with the perfect view of green fields, leafless vines and distant rolling green hills covered in gumtrees. Liz knew the sunrises would have been spectacular.

The furniture was expensive rattan mixed with imported teak pieces and the floor looked like polished slate. Apart from the photos, the walls were covered with indigenous art, which never came cheaply and various cultural pieces from Fiji or other Pacific Islands.

'You had it tough.' Liz made the statement with a knowing tone and the woman looked at her again.

'She ran away at sixteen when I told her we were going to live in the Aboriginal community. I took the position there because it guaranteed me any placement I wanted after I did the regional community work. I took the job for her, for a better life, but she didn't see it that way. In the end, I loved my time there, but it cost me my daughter because I had to let Narelle go and work out what she wanted to do with her life. She wouldn't listen to me anymore.'

'Have you seen her much since?'

'She used to visit for special occasions, Christmas, Easter, that type of thing. The twins loved her to bits, but she never felt like she belonged. Strange really, considering it should have been the twins who felt like foreigners away from their tribe.'

'You said she used to visit.'

There was a long silence as Ms Fergusson composed herself. 'I've not seen Narelle for at least five years.'

'Ms Fergusson, we understand you had Narelle while you were involved with the outlaw motorcycle gang, the Harlequins. Is that correct?'

'It is.'

'Is Narelle's father a bikie gang member?'

'No. Why?'

'Because she was working in a Harlequins' bar when she went missing and we think her disappearance is linked to a case the police are working on with bikie connections.'

'Her father wasn't a bikie. He was one of their connections, a big one.' Max and Liz exchanged looks. 'He wouldn't hurt Narelle, not in a million years.'

'Does he know about her?'

'He does, but I never asked him for anything. He's married and high profile. He gave me some cash, years back, to help with my education and that was it.'

'Did the Harlequins know you were pregnant? Did one of them have reason to believe they were Narelle's father?'

'Possibly. Look, if Narelle is in trouble, I'll do what I can to help her, but I'm not giving up her father's name, you understand?'

25

Liz looked at the notes she'd made from their visit with Ms Fergusson. She carried her hot coffee mug between her hands, hugging it for warmth and taking a sip as she turned the thermostat up on the underfloor heating.

She returned to her tablet and sent the notes via email so she could read them on her computer. She pulled out her mobile and dialled. It was answered on the third ring.

'Liz. What's up?'

'Jenny. Can you run a few names for me?'

'Sure. I'm still at work, I'll punch them in now. Just let me get the right screen open.' Liz waited as Jenny clicked keys on her computer. She could hear the background office noise of phones and voices.

'Okay, who you got?'

'Sebastian Muller and Ryan Mitchell. Both full badge Harlequins members in the eighties.'

The keys clicked again and Liz took another sip of her coffee.

'What am I checking for?'

'Narelle's mum said she was shacking up with both when she got pregnant. She says neither is the dad, but they might think they are.'

'Oh, interesting. Muller is dead, died in a drive-by shooting in Perth presumed to be done by a rival gang, the Renegades by the looks. Mitchell is inside. Armed robbery and aggravated assault. Been there for over four years.'

'Okay, so neither of them had anything to do with Narelle's disappearance or Braithwaite's death.'

'Jack told you about Rickard, right?'

'He did. Any idea where Narelle would be hiding? We need to speak with her and find out just how tight she and Rickard were.'

'Johnnie was asking questions today. I'm not sure if he's as innocent as he appears, but either he's been helping his partner commit felonies or he knows about them and doesn't know how to handle the knowledge.'

'He thinks Rickard is dirty?'

'That or *he* is dirty and he's sticking Rickard in the shit for it, but it was Rickard who has the limp and was seen in Narelle's apartment, not Johnnie.'

'We are missing something. We really need to find where Narelle is. She's the missing link in all of this. I've got a hunch. Can you ask Penny to run Narelle's DNA? She must have something from the apartment?'

'Sure, what are we running it against? There was no DNA left on Braithwaite's body and nothing at Jack's place.'

'I want paternal DNA.'

'Whose?'

'I can't say on the phone. I'll text you a name.'

'O…kay? Any word on the video?'

'I'm chasing Scott now. He'll only just be waking up.'

'I'll organise the DNA test. You let me know what the video turns up.'

'Will do.' Liz hung up and sent the message to Jenny with the name of the DNA sample she wanted her to check Narelle against. It wasn't a name to be said aloud on the phone.

She put her phone down and opened her laptop, forwarding the video to Scott before checking work emails. Today wasn't her rostered day, but she still needed to keep her own diary under control.

She searched for Ted's email address but only found the message he'd sent before their last meeting. Strange, she had expected to hear from him again before he left town, but maybe he had a new, younger Lillian to play with. She closed her computer and started on dinner.

****

Jenny looked at her phone and read the text. She took a sharp breath and wondered how Liz had come up with that name. Then she thought about what she'd seen on the photo of the younger Narelle. Either way, the girl had a nose like a bloodhound so she wasn't about to argue with her.

She used the internal desk phone and called Penny. The phone rang out and she tried the main extension. Rodriguez answered.

'Forensics.'

'Hey Fernando.' Jenny kept the tone light. Jack and Max had suspicions, especially after finding out about the Harlequins case and evidence chain issues, but he didn't need to know any of that.

'Hi Detective. What can I do for you?'

'Is Penny in?'

'No, left about ten minutes ago. Anything I can help with?'

'No, personal girl stuff. I'll catch her up soon.'

'Okay.'

Jenny grabbed her bag out of the drawer, holstered her gun and put her jacket on. She pressed the computer off as she rushed from the office and down the stairs. She was almost to the foyer when she ran into Anderson.

'Just the person I'm looking for.' Jenny looked up into his dark brown eyes and went to dodge around him.

'I'm trying to catch up with someone.' She took off, but he grabbed her arm and pulled her back. 'Hey,' she objected, giving him a cold stare.

'We need to talk.' He pushed her against the wall of the stairs. Jenny cringed. If anyone from her department saw them, chins would start wagging, rapidly. Besides, he'd been all stealth only a day ago. What had changed?

'Not here.' The stairs weren't that busy, most took the elevator, but Anderson should have known better. Jenny pushed him back with the flat of her hand.

'You keep saying that.' He wiggled his eyebrows and Jenny couldn't help but think of Groucho Marks.

She decided the DNA would have to wait. 'What do you want?'

'Coffee.' He grabbed her arm and led her down the stairs. 'You got my message?'

'That depends, I get a lot of messages, but none from you that I know of.'

'*Watch* it Williams.' He emphasised the first word.

'I thought that was you. Why the cloak and dagger?' They moved out into the street and started walking. Jenny didn't realise the direction straight away, but when she did, she stopped. 'Where are we going?'

'Your place.'

'The fact you know where I live is disturbing.' He made a *'doesn't everyone'* gesture. 'But since you know, then you'll also be aware I have a roommate so covert conversations won't work there.'

'Your roommate isn't home.'

'Oh my god. You're spying on me!'

'You are worth spying on.' He grinned and Jenny rolled her eyes.

'That's your idea of a pick up? What's wrong with your place?'

'I live with my mum.' Jenny laughed, loudly.

'Really!'

'She's got dementia.' Jenny stopped walking again.

'Oh, shit. I'm sorry. You seem to know a lot more about me than I do about you.'

'It's okay, we have some extra help when I'm at work, but,' he shrugged, 'let's say the personal life isn't quite the same.'

Anderson hadn't let go of Jenny's arm and she only now realised it. The warmth of his body so close was distracting as they walked the two blocks to her apartment.

'Why didn't you just give me the video at the gym?'

'I don't know how deep the leak goes. I'm certain I'm being watched and I *know* your department is.'

'So why are you on this anyway? The Bikie Task Force investigating a Major Crimes leak? Isn't that a job for Internal Affairs?'

'It's complicated but when the Judge was poisoned, the bikie gangs closed ranks. Then Jack got caught with drugs. The bikies were already reeling. All hell could have broken loose, so I went in hard on your department and the investigation, hoping to make the gangs think I was focussed on your department. In truth, I was, because I thought Jack was dirty like his old man. But my guys on the inside said Jack was clean and you started digging in deep to prove it. That's when I knew you were okay.'

'Sooo glad I'm in the club but that doesn't explain why you pulled the Braithwaite case out from under me.'

'At first we thought Braithwaite's murder was the Bikies retaliating. But then we realised there was no gang connection and if Jack wasn't dirty, who was? Who had planted the drugs on him and who had killed Braithwaite, a known gang affiliate? I had to treat everyone in your department as hostile.' Anderson stopped outside Jenny's apartment building before nodding for her to lead the way.

She rounded on him at the elevator as he backed her into the wall. 'Hostile is a good word for your behaviour Detective.'

'You aren't exactly one to talk. Your bedside manner can't be described as sweet either.' He was breathing warm air near Jenny's ear and her heart fluttered, despite her mind telling her he was a big, macho oaf and she should kick him in the nuts.

'I don't have bedside manner.' She found her voice. 'I'm a detective, not a doctor. If you know Jack is clean, why haven't you reinstated him?'

'Because I need to find the person who planted the drugs, the real leak and keeping Jack on suspension has given me more help than I would have gotten otherwise.'

Jenny pushed him away, turning on him and pinning him to the wall. She knew he was letting her.

'You are using me, Max and, and....' Jenny didn't say Liz. She shook her head and pressed the elevator button.

'And his friend. Yes. Fox Investigations. Free consultancy. It's pretty handy.' Anderson grinned.

'You really are a shithead you know. Who called in the tip?'

'We traced it to a pay phone. Who the hell uses a pay phone these days?'

'Someone who doesn't want to be traced, obviously.' The elevator doors opened and Jenny got in, hesitating about letting Anderson follow her up, but she had to get as much information as possible. At least that was how she rationalised the situation.

He stepped in and pressed the tenth floor. She rolled her eyes again. *Of course he knows which floor I live on.*

'You're just giving me the inspiration I needed to get my own place you know.' He laughed, the sound making Jenny's stomach flutter. *Oh for fuck's sake girl, get a grip.* She crossed her arms over her chest and leant back against the elevator wall.

The defensive behaviour wasn't lost on Anderson, who moved closer, his posture the complete opposite of Jenny's.

'Fox got their IT guy on the video yet?' He scanned her body with his eyes, his conversation not matching the look on his face.

'How the hell….' She shook her head and shoved him to the other side of the elevator, giving her breathing room. 'You gave me the video to clean it up for you? What! Departmental cuts making it too hard for your team to manage?'

'Yours will be faster. Don't you want to get Jack back to work as soon as possible?'

'Of course I do,' she sighed. He was right of course, but she still didn't know if she could really trust him. The elevator doors opened and Jenny stepped out. The idea she shouldn't let him into her apartment crossed her mind. Anderson must have read her body language. He moved out of the elevator without giving her a chance to send him back down.

'Then your team should be happy to help me nail this bastard.'

Jenny sighed as she got her keys out of her bag and opened her front door. 'Where was the payphone anyway?'

She waved Anderson into the apartment before following. She barely had time to slam the door closed with her foot and throw her bag down on the small side table before Anderson pinned her to the back of the door.

'You are hot and you know it, don't you!' He held both her hands with his against the door, leaning in closely so his lips were almost touching hers.

Jenny didn't know what to say. Her mind was racing between resisting his advances, pushing him for information or devouring him.

Anderson moved in for a kiss, but stopped short, a confident grin making Jenny's mind up for her.

'Get off me before I cause you permanent damage.' Jenny's knee caressed his groin menacingly.

'You don't really want to do that.' He looked down and then back up with questioning eyes.

Jenny shrugged as best she could with her hands still trapped against the door. 'You're over confident Detective. It's not an asset.'

'It usually is.' He didn't loosen his hold, but Jenny wasn't fighting him either. His lips still hovered above hers. Her mind screamed no, but her body said yes. 'The phone booth was on Halifax Street.' He released her hands and moved into the small kitchen.

'Shit!'

'That mean something to you?' He turned to watch her expression.

Jenny grabbed her phone out of her pocket and started typing a group text.

26

Liz read the text and took a long deep breath. She tapped out a return text to everyone in the group message and waited, her eyes hovering over the screen in suspense. Things were starting to make some sense, but there were still so many questions unanswered.

Jenny's reply came first. *Be there as soon as I can. Can I bring an extra?* Liz frowned and wondered who the extra might be. Letting more people know where she lived wasn't high on her priority list.

Not at my place, sorry Jen.

I think he needs to be in on this. Where else can we meet?

Liz had a pretty good idea who the extra was now. She typed back. *Nino's in an hour. I'll book.* The text went to everyone.

Max had already answered Jenny's initial text with a wide eyed yellow 'wow' face and Jack had yet to reply.

Liz booked the table for five people and checked her emails. It was likely too early for Scott to be working, but she hoped he'd seen the emailed video.

She scanned her emails and found more spam than anything useful. She looked at her watch and tapped her fingers on the kitchen counter, the sound drummed against the stone. She dialled Scott's number, hoping she wasn't waking him up. He preferred to work at night, but she had no idea what time he got up to start.

'Liz. I'm on it. I promise.'

'Sorry Scott. Didn't mean to hassle you, it's just a few things in this case are coming together and that video is one of the last pieces.'

'Well it's not the movies. Cleaning up grainy security camera footage isn't as easy as the click of a few buttons. The camera is focused on the person at the ATM so the image of the person on Jack's balcony is not good quality. Plus, most new cameras record in high def, 1080p and that's good for blowing up images and getting good stills, but this camera must be in an older ATM because it's very pixelated. Trying to zoom in, and clean up the image is going to take some time.'

'I'm sorry to put you under the pump. Send me a message and a screenshot as soon as you find anything. I'll double the hourly rate on this one if it helps.'

'Money can't buy me a better image to work with Liz. I'll do my best no matter what. You'll be the first to know.'

Liz sighed as she packed her phone in her backpack and changed, ready for dinner. Jack still hadn't responded and it was making her a little uneasy. She hadn't spoken to him since the morning, on the way to Ms Fergusson's place.

****

Jack felt his phone vibrate in his pocket but ignored it, his eyes were fixed on his target. The circumstantial evidence they had on Rickard wasn't enough for Jenny to bring a Major Crimes detective in for questioning. They needed more. Running surveillance on Rickard was his best chance of finding what they needed.

Jack watched him empty the garbage and roll the wheelie bin out to the curb. His limp was still evident and Jack felt the bile rise in his throat. *Why the hell was Rickard in his apartment? Did he plant the drugs the first time?*

Rickard went back inside and Jack waited a while. The light came on in the front room and Jack watched the shadows move behind the curtains as Rickard sat down. He moved closer to the house and heard the television come on. The local news theme drummed loudly and once Jack was confident Rickard had settled in to watch it, he moved to the rubbish bin. He didn't need a search warrant to go through the garbage now it was on council land.

Jack looked over his shoulder as he opened the bin. He could hardly go through it in the street so he was relieved to see that at least the guy used garbage bags. He pulled the last two out of the bin and moved off the street and around the corner to where his car was parked.

He opened the boot and tossed the bags in, wiping his hands on a gym towel before closing the boot. He pulled his phone out of his pocket as he got into the driver's seat of his car. He went to put his key in the ignition as he read the message, but stopped. Had they been chasing the wrong person? Had she played them for fools?

He replied to the text to agree to meet. The garbage would have to wait. He smiled as he imagined Max's face when he told him he needed a hand to search Rickards's rubbish. 'Just like old times,' he said aloud as he put the key in and turned to start the car.

Ten minutes later Jack found a park, pulled out his Police Permit and clicked the lock button on his keys. The restaurant was busy, but not packed and he spotted his group at the back, in a corner away from other patrons.

There was an extra person he hadn't been expecting and Jack studied the broad shoulders on the man's back as he approached. It was winter and the weather had been less than pleasant, but this guy wore a white, tight fitting tee shirt that revealed traditional tattoos down his arm. Anderson, why the hell was Anderson at this meeting? He moved past the bulky figure to the other side of the rectangular table to sit between Max and Liz.

'Sorry I'm late. Got tied up.' He didn't want to elaborate as he watched Anderson's expression closely. The guy looked like he was trying to be friendly. Jack didn't know him well, but his Pitbull reputation preceded him and the few times they'd crossed paths, it had never been amicable. Friendly was never a word used in the same sentence as Task Force Senior Detective Anderson.

'Jack. You know Anderson,' Jenny offered an introduction. Jack nodded.

'We've crossed paths.' The statement made Liz look to Max, a question in her expression. He tipped his head to his shoulder with a one-arm shrug and Liz sighed.

'Jack.' Anderson nodded as understanding passed between them.

'He's been helping on our case,' Jenny continued, trying to relieve the obvious tension between the two men.

'Has he?' Jack poured a wine from the open bottle in the middle of the table and took a sip. Not usually a fan of Lambrusco, he wasn't about to be fussy right now.

'The tip-off call came from a Halifax phone booth Jack.' Anderson gave me the information,' Jenny pushed.

'After he withheld it for what, a week?' Jack took another long sip of wine.

'I ordered you some pasta,' Liz interrupted, trying to defuse the situation before it escalated.

'And you've never withheld information until you knew who you were dealing with, hey Jack.' Anderson was smiling but it wasn't reaching his eyes.

'You've been using us. You've jeopardised my career for your own entertainment.' Jack knew he sounded hollow, even to his own ears.

'Jack. Look at me.' Liz tapped his hand gently and Jack felt the warmth of her touch. He fought to keep his penetrating gaze on Anderson, but Liz tapped his hand once more.

He let his stare drop, his eyes locking with Liz's. 'We are on the same team now. Hear him out, okay?'

Jack could feel the rage inside. He didn't know why. Was it his father nearly dying? Was it that he thought his mum might have tried to kill him? He hadn't voiced his suspicions aloud. Was that the problem? Was it just pent-up frustration?

Jack finally nodded. 'What pasta did you order?'

Liz smiled and tapped his hand once more before releasing it. Jack felt the warmth evaporate and missed it instantly.

'Bolognaise. Always a safe option for a meat eater. I can change it though. Nino won't mind.'

'No Bolognaise is fine. Thanks.'

'So, where are we at?' Max called the meeting to order and everyone laughed. It was an ice breaking, nervous giggle moment and they all knew it, but it was a start.

'Look, I've kept my cards close for a reason. If it wasn't for your dedicated colleague here,' Anderson nodded to Jenny, 'I'd still have them close. This case has led down a rabbit hole from the moment it hit my desk.'

'What case? Jack's drug charges?' Max took a swig of his beer. Jack kept himself under control at the mention of the charges against him.

'No, this case has been building for ages. I can't say too much, but you all know about Jack's dad's history. Well it crosses over with the local bikie gangs, decades ago. When the drugs turned up at Jack's place, well we thought the apple hadn't fallen far from the tree.' Anderson put up his hand as Max began to protest. 'Don't worry, he's in the clear but I couldn't let anyone know that. We needed whoever set him up to think we still suspected him.'

'So, I was right, you've been using me?'

'Not just you Jack,' Jenny added. 'Don't worry, I'll make him pay for it, but Anderson has been using us all to dig the guts out of this case.'

'And you're nearly there. Look, it's too deep for me to go into, but you know what undercover work is like. You start to wonder if your detectives have gone off script. I didn't know who to trust on this one. A Judge, a senior detective, a departmental leak and bikie links. You can see it from my point of view, right!'

Jack could. He understood he would likely have done the exact same thing if it were his case, but he didn't like being on the receiving end of the rationale.

He nodded for Anderson to go on. 'Jenny brought me in after I shared where the anonymous tip-off to raid your place came from. Apparently, it resonated with your team.'

'Sure. The bar where we think my dad was poisoned is on Halifax Street. It means that the guy we thought was involved, Braithwaite, shouldn't have been our suspect at all. His girlfriend works at the bar. We all made the mistake of thinking she had no stake in this.'

'She has no motive we know of,' Max offered, taking another sip of his beer as Nino arrived and placed a plate in front of Liz, then Jenny. The girls thanked him and the conversation stopped until the rest of the plates were distributed.

Jack's stomach grumbled as the aroma of Bolognaise hit his nostrils. He hadn't realised how hungry he was. Liz had chicken risotto and Jenny had a huge pizza with basil and Neapolitan sauce, topped with fetta. She was a carb machine and he smiled wistfully remembering when he could eat like that.

'Well, Narelle *could* have a motive.' Jenny stated, then stopped when she looked at Liz. Jack hadn't seen the silent exchange, but he searched Liz's features when Jenny hesitated. She was keeping something from him.

'I checked the files and the case that Rickard busted her on, your dad resided over.' Jenny continued. Jack could tell it wasn't what she'd originally planned to share, but it was something of interest.

'So you think Narelle tried to kill my dad because he was the Judge on her solicitation case? That's a bit thin, isn't it?' Jack looked around the table for confirmation.

'Well it's likely where she forged a relationship with Rickard. He's in this up to his neck. Time to grill Johnnie I think?' Max cut into his thick steak, the juice oozed out into the creamy basil pesto sauce and fried chips.

'Jenny can't really question Johnnie yet. We have no evidence Rickard is involved except his past booking of a prostitute,' Anderson declared before returning to his vegetarian basil pasta dish. The choice surprised Jack. The guy was built like the proverbial brick shithouse and he assumed he must have lived on protein. Maybe it was protein powder that built that bulk.

'I can bail him up.' Max's grin was sinister and Jack smiled. Anderson on the other hand looked like he was going to protest.

Jack intervened. 'Look. I've grabbed Rickard's garbage, maybe we'll find something to pursue there.'

'Without a warrant!' Anderson shook his head.

'Don't be a dick. It's not my first day at the dance Anderson. It was on the footpath, out in the wheelie bin on council land, ready for pick up. I took the top two bags and threw them in the boot. You're welcome to go through them with me.' Jack fully expected a blanket no, but Anderson surprised him again.

'Sure. As soon as we are done here.'

Jack exchanged a look with Max who shrugged. Normally he would have bailed on the duty, but something about

Anderson's willingness was a challenge to his old partner. Jack could see it in Max's eyes.

'I'm in.' Anderson grinned knowingly.

'Okay, no more rubbish talk during dinner.' Liz shuddered. 'Where would Narelle be? Any ideas anyone? She's not with her mum. Rickard is obviously looking for her and she took off so he wouldn't find her. Where else would she go?'

'The bar maybe?' Jenny said before taking a sip of her wine. 'This is really nice. I can see why you eat here so often Liz.'

'Well I usually come here for breakfast and morning coffee, dinner occasionally, but since you lot came along I seem to live here.' Everyone laughed and Liz raised her glass to toast.

'To new friends and catching bad guys.' Her glass chimed with Jack's and he felt his stomach roll.

'And bad girls.' Jenny added and Jack somehow thought of Liz in fishnet stockings and a G-string. Her brow rose as if she were reading his mind, so he tipped his head and turned his glass to Max's hovering beer bottle.

'Any word on the video?' Anderson asked and Jack's question about the source was revealed. Maybe he wasn't so bad afterall?

'Not yet. Scott is working on it but he said it's pretty poor quality.' Liz stirred her risotto as she spoke. Jack noticed she rarely finished a meal. Max seemed to always be ready to pick up the left overs. He reminded Jack of a family dog, minus the drool.

As if reading his mind, she placed her fork down on the plate and looked to see if Max was finished. They hadn't been married for decades, but maybe old habits were hard to break.

'Do you want this?'

'Does a fish pee in water?' Max held out his plate for Liz and took hers. Jack leant back to give them room. He couldn't eat while plates were moving over his anyway.

He looked up and Jenny was grinning sheepishly at Anderson and he frowned. *Were they involved?* He shook his head. None of his business he reminded himself.

'Okay. We'll go through the rubbish from Rickard's and see if anything sticks out. Max can follow Johnnie tomorrow and if the opportunity arises, quiz him on Rickard and Narelle.' Everyone nodded.

'I'll follow up with Scott later tonight and see what he can find. In the meantime, Jenny, can you chase up all Narelle's known associates? Where is she hiding out? She's now our number one suspect since she worked around the corner from the phone box where Anderson's anonymous call came from.' Liz was all business once more and Jack marvelled at her organisational skills.

'I could do with you all on my team fulltime.' Anderson fixed Liz with a gaze and Jack could tell he was thinking of saying more. Maybe about her *other* occupation, maybe just a general comment, but he must have thought better of it as he turned to Jack. 'Where are we going through this garbage? Can't be at the station, you're still on suspension.'

'Ha ha.' Jack rolled his eyes at the lame joke. 'Max's place. Neutral ground.'

'I don't want all that rubbish off-loaded at my place.' Max protested.

'Why not? It will fit right in.'

'Oooh that's just below the belt mate.' Max punched Jack in the arm. 'I've tidied up since you were last over. My new job and all.'

'New job my arse. You were just afraid Jackie might come over unannounced.' Jack punched him back.

'Nothing to do with it.' Max finished Liz's risotto and belched under his breath. 'See.' Jack couldn't hold back the full bellied laugh. Max obviously thought a silent belch was a step up from an audible one.

'Mate!' Jack shook his head and watched Anderson question Jenny with his eyes. She shrugged as if their behaviour was normal practice, but he seemed less than satisfied.

'Jackie is our daughter.' Liz offered to at least deal with one unanswered question.

Anderson looked from Max to Liz, his mouth wide as Jenny tapped him on the shoulder conciliatorily. 'It's okay, you've got a lot to catch up on.'

Another round of laughter but this time, Anderson wasn't joining in.

27

Max opened the door on his small, one bedroom unit. The air smelt musty, the carpet well past its use-by date. He threw his keys on the warn melamine counter and grabbed three beers from his fridge before returning to the front porch.

There was no way he was going to go through rubbish in his own home. He checked to see that his mobile had plenty of charge before putting it back in his pocket. He'd need to take photos on his phone if they found anything.

Jack walked up the driveway with Anderson. There wasn't a lot of spare parking at his unit block. The building took up nearly the entire allotment, with one car park and one visitor park per unit. With a few couples in the complex which was full of one-bedroom apartments, there wasn't much in the way of visitor parking spots left.

'I shouldn't have another. I've got to drive home Max,' Jack protested as his former partner handed him an already open beer.

'You can hang around until it wears off. You only had a few glasses at dinner, you'll be right mate.'

'Famous last words.' Anderson took the offered beer despite his comment, before taking a polite sip and placing it on the cracked brick wall around the overgrown garden outside Max's unit.

'Where do you want to go through these?' Jack held up two black bags in one hand. The plastic rustled as he shook them gently.

'The big bins are around back. We'll do it there and put it all straight in the bulk bins as we go.' Max started moving off the cracked and buckling concrete walkway and onto the pot-holed bitumen driveway that led to the rear of the unit block.

'Makes sense.' Jack followed, beer in hand. Anderson picked his drink up and joined them.

'I'm not sure I can keep up with you two.' He saluted with the open beer stubby and Max laughed.

'What! I always thought you Kiwis were built to take it.'

'Nah mate. Give me a bowl of Kava and I'll likely come out on top, but this stuff isn't what I grew up on.'

'Really? I thought our Kiwi cousins were big beer drinkers.' Jack put the bags of garbage down next to the red-topped wheelie bins and undid the first one, tipping the contents onto the ground. There wasn't a lot of light in the parking lot, so both Max and Jack flicked on torches, shortly followed by Anderson.

'Probably should have done this in the morning you know.' Max stated the obvious.

'Some of us have other jobs to get to.' Anderson took a pen out of his pocket and dropped down to his haunches. 'A lot of Kiwis drink beer, but personally I'm only a social drinker and I prefer wine over beer. My dad's Fijian. I grew up following some of his traditions and Kava was one that stuck.'

'Not a beer drinker. That's sacrilege,' Max chuckled. 'I lost count of how many generations my family have been here. It's just pure Aussie to drink beer. I guess I really should consider cutting down, but I only just gave up smoking. I think the beer might have to wait.'

'Good on you.' Anderson offered as he pushed a condom and some dental floss to the side. 'Do we bother with DNA on this?' He pointed to the used condom and Max and Jack screwed up their noses.

'Maybe worth it if he is sleeping with Narelle. Might go to motive or maybe a reason to pull him in for questioning.'

159

Anderson nodded and pulled a pair of gloves and a zip lock bag out of his back pocket. 'Max, can you grab a happy snap?'

'Sure.' Max opened his camera on the phone and set the flash on. He took a photo of the pile in front of them, then the piece of evidence they were bagging. The flash in the darkness must have alerted the neighbours, that or their voices had.

'What the fuck is going on here? Piss off or I'm calling the police.' It was his nosey old neighbour. He shone his torch in her direction and her hands flew up to her eyes. At least her hair wasn't in curlers today.

'We *are* the police. It's all fine Meredith. Go back inside.'

'That you Max. Bloody hell, you scared the crap out of me.'

'See you later Meredith.' Max dismissed the old lady, thankful it was a cold night or she would have stood over them, supervising. She totted off to her unit and all the flash-lights came back to bear on the pile of rubbish. Nothing else of interest turned up in the first bag, so they piled it all into the big wheelie bin and started on bag number two.

'He's a detective. He would have to be a moron to leave evidence in his own rubbish bin.' Max pushed some vegetable scraps away from a Charcoal Chicken bag and gagged. The smell was putrid and he was thankful it wasn't summer or the thing would have been wriggling with maggots. The summer flies were ruthless in Adelaide.

'You'd think so, but you'd also be surprised what we find.' Anderson had made the comment casually but both torches fell on his face before he realised what he'd said.

'You investigate for Internal Affairs often?' Jack's tone was less than amused.

'I used to. I've been with the Bikie Task Force for five years now, but I was with IA before that.'

'Nice.' Max's tone wasn't nice at all.

'Someone has to do it. There are plenty of dirty cops out there.' Anderson didn't sound defensive, in fact he sounded quite proud. Max frowned in the darkness. His own reputation was less than squeaky clean and he wondered if Anderson had a file on him. He concluded he likely did.

'They aren't all murderers.' He tried not to sound defensive.

'Nope, they aren't but cops shouldn't be above the law.'

'You sound like Jack. You two would make a lovely couple.' Max returned his attention to the pile of rubbish.

The silence wasn't lost on their new-found friend. Max knew the guy's cogs would have been turning, trying to work out what Max was so pissed off about.

'I grew up in a poor part of town, but we were always happy. Family means everything to my people. The only thing more important than family is integrity. Sorry if I sound like a pious dick, but that's just the way I am. That's why I chose the Bikie Task Force—drugs, sex trade, demoralising women and extortion are just the bottom of the pit as far as I'm concerned.'

'He gets it Anderson.' Jack put his hand on Anderson's shoulder. 'Let's focus on the case.'

'Hemi. It's my first name, just call me Hemi, thanks.'

'Hemi it is.'

'Shit!' All the flash lights moved to join Max's on the rubbish pile.

'It's not much, but it's enough to bring him in for questioning.' Anderson lifted the coaster up as Max took a photo, then he placed it in another zip lock bag.

'I think that's a wrap boys.' Max placed his camera in his pocket and patted Anderson on the shoulder, as if to say *no hard feelings*.

****

Liz opened her email and checked her phone. No text or message from Scott yet. She sighed and checked her Foxy Escort account to see if she needed to follow up with anything. It was Connie's roster, but Liz had trouble truly letting go of the helm.

She wondered again why Ted hadn't emailed her. Apart from seeing her again before he left, he always sent a thank you email after one of their "dates". She thought about the mysterious stalker who pretended to be one of Ted's friends and puzzled over why he'd bothered to seek her out. She'd heard nothing more from him and the photo Jenny had obtained of him didn't turn up any leads. Any normal client she rejected would have sent an enraged email, it was what usually happened, but nothing had come through.

When her phone rang, Liz jumped. She'd been so focused on her emails and her thoughts that the sound startled her.

'Scott. Glad to hear from you.'

'You don't know if I've got good news or not yet.'

'Whatever you have, I know you've done your best.' Liz hoped his best was enough, but said nothing.

'It's not perfect, but at least we have a few features. Female, about five foot eight by the height of the door, window etc, but other than build and basic hair colour, I can't give you much else. I'll send the photos through now.'

Liz tried not to sound disappointed. 'Thanks Scott. I'm sure we can make something from it.'

'I hope so. Talk soon. Stay safe.' The phone line went dead and Liz stared at the screen, waiting for the photos to appear. A text arrived and she rolled her eyes. *Check your email.*

He must have been watching her through the damned laptop camera. She knew he wasn't but it felt like it. The tech wasn't outside his scope.

Photos sent via text were compressed. She needed a full resolution one so she could zoom in as much as possible. She refreshed her email account for Fox Investigations and waited.

The email arrived after the third refresh and she opened the first attachment. It was far from conclusive, but could have easily been Narelle. The balcony lighting was shocking, but the hair that poked out of the hoodie was blonde. Narelle had blonde hair. The build was right, the height Scott had estimated was spot on too. Was it enough to get a warrant for her arrest? Probably not, but they should at least be able to get a BOLO out that she was wanted for questioning.

'Where are you Narelle?' Liz said aloud as she began a text to Jack, then checked her watch and changed her mind. Dialling his number, she took a deep breath, remembering how angry he was at dinner until she calmed him down. Then the look he had given her afterward. Was she making more of it than was intended?

'Liz, everything okay?'

'Yes Detective. I'm not in any trouble, yet.' She smiled and he chuckled. 'I've got the photos back from Scott.'

'That's great. We've found a bar coaster from Rosie's in Rickard's rubbish so that's enough to interview him, well Jenny and Anderson will do the interview, but Rickard will be brought in tomorrow for questioning.'

'That's good news. The photos are not conclusive. Your break and enterer was definitely a female, about Narelle's height and build with blonde hair. All very circumstantial I'm sure, but maybe enough for Jenny to issue a BOLO that she is wanted for questioning.'

'That's great work Liz. I'll see if Jenny can get Crime Watch to put Narelle's photo on the news. She'll chase up any known associates tomorrow.' There was a short silence, as though Jack wanted to say more, but didn't.

'We are getting there Liz.'

'We are Jack. Talk soon.' Liz hung up before she could invite him over, before he could say no.

28

Jenny rolled over as her alarm clock sounded. She felt like she'd had a whole three hours of sleep. Today was going to be huge. Questioning another cop, that was a big deal for the probationary detective and although she wasn't about to admit it, she was feeling a little overwhelmed.

Without Jack along to lead the questioning, she was experiencing a little anxiety. Anderson would be there, but showing weakness in front of the Task Force detective wasn't an option. Jenny didn't do vulnerable. Ever.

As if his ears were burning, Jack's name flashed up on her mobile screen which was still set to silent. 'Jack. What's happening?'

'You doing okay?'

Jenny laughed nervously and hoped it didn't sound that way. 'I'm okay. Didn't get a lot of sleep, that's all.'

'You've got this Detective Williams.' The reference to her official work title bolstered her spirits. The boss had her back.

'Thanks Boss.'

'Keep me posted.'

'Of course. You'll be the first to know anything. I'll run through Narelle's priors and known associates. We'll find her.'

'About that. Liz got the photos from Scott. You'll have a copy in your work email by now. Nothing solid, but Narelle is still a likely for the B and E, not just the anonymous tip-off. Get a BOLO out on her, on the news, you know the drill. Wanted for questioning in connection to, that type of thing.'

'You got it. Thanks.'

'For what?'

'For trusting me.'

Jack laughed. 'You know I trust you Jenny, but while your mate keeps me on suspension, I can't do shit. I feel hamstrung.'

'I hate to agree with him, but until we find Narelle, it's probably the best option of flushing her out. Any idea why she'd set you up though?'

There was a short silence. No one had really considered the motive. 'No idea.'

'I'll be in touch soon.' Jenny hung up, wondering if Liz's bloodhound nose was right and made a mental note to chase up Penny and the DNA results as soon as she got a spare minute. Keeping it from Jack wasn't her preferred choice, but it was Liz's call.

Twenty minutes later the detective flew out the door with a piece of toast in her mouth and her mobile virtually attached to her ear.

'No, I can pick up a patrol car.' Jenny insisted through a half-full mouth. 'I'm already outside.' Jenny sighed as she exited the foyer of her building to find Anderson parked in a No Parking zone just in front of the bus stop outside her apartment building.

He waved her over and she opened the passenger door and got in, holding the last bit of toast in her mouth as she pulled the seat belt on. She kept the toast there while she pulled back her hair and put it into a long, low-set pony tail.

Out of the corner of her eye she saw Anderson grinning as he drove the car away from the curb and into the early morning traffic. 'What?'

'You look adorable with a mouthful of toast.'

She pulled the toast out with a scowl. 'Oh shut up,' she retorted, before taking another snapping bite and chewing it menacingly.

'Let's bring Detective Rickard in, hey.'

'How do you know he wasn't coming in to work today anyway?'

'Jack said he's still limping. He wouldn't risk you asking too many questions. He knows you're a sharp one.'

Jenny couldn't decide if he was taking the piss, but finally decided he wasn't. 'Since when have you and Jack become bosom buddies? I thought he was going to rip your head off at dinner until Liz calmed him down.'

'Yeah, what was with that anyway?'

'You've left him on the bench on purpose.'

'No, not that. Liz and him?'

'Ah, the four-hundred-million-dollar question. It's complicated. Don't change the subject. Anyway, did you two bond over garbage duty or something?'

'Something like that.'

Jenny sighed. 'You'll need to do better than that.'

Anderson grinned. 'You're a seriously good interrogator you know.' Jenny tried to hide a grin at his Kiwi accent on the word pronounced as *sirusly* but changed quickly to a pout as he took his eyes off the road to look her way.

He sighed in resignation. 'I told him his record would be cleaned up as soon as I explained he'd been working undercover and that the drug bust was just a cover.'

'You said that?'

'I did.'

'*When* will you clear it up?'

'Soon. We need to pull these pieces together first. I don't want anyone thinking Jack's aiding in the investigation. Especially not Rickard or his partner.'

'Makes sense. Are we questioning Johnnie too? He probably knows something.'

'Probably.'

Jenny suddenly remembered Penny and pulled out her mobile. 'Excuse me a sec. I just need to check on some pathology.'

The phone rang three times before Penny picked up. 'Police Forensic Unit. Penny Butler speaking.'

'Penny, it's Jenny. Any update on that DNA?'

'I only just got in, give me a second.' Jenny could hear papers shuffling as Penny moved things around her desk. Keys tapped on her keyboard before she picked the receiver back up. 'Bingo. Tell Liz she was spot on.'

'That answers a few questions. Thanks Penny.' Jenny hung up and dialled Liz. She looked at Anderson who was driving, making his way through traffic, politely not speculating or saying a word. She knew the questions would come after she finished on the phone, but this wasn't her story to tell, not yet anyway.

'Jenny.' Liz answered.

'Hey Liz, Penny got those results you were chasing. I'm on my way to pick up Rickard with Anderson, but I thought you'd want to know. You were right.'

Jenny heard a quick intake of breath as Liz digested what a yes meant. 'Thanks Jenny.'

'What's the plan?' Jenny really wanted to know what Liz intended to do with the information.

'I think it's about time I got to know Jack's mum and dad, don't you?'

'Is that a good idea?'

'Probably not, but I need to ask Judge Bruce Cunningham a few questions.'

'You should let Max know first. If you get yourself into any more trouble, both Jack and Max won't let you out of their sight again.'

'I doubt a man in a wheelchair can do me any damage Jenny. I'll be fine. Talk soon.' The phone went dead and Jenny stared at the screen, avoiding Anderson's sideways glances.

'Anything I should know about?'

'Not before Max and Jack. Liz says no, so no it is.'

'You take orders from an amateur PI and high-class Madam now?'

'I do when it concerns Jack.'

29

Liz got dressed, put on some light foundation and neutral toned lipstick before grabbing her Prada backpack and Moncler hooded down jacket. The winter's day was bleak and the drizzle had not let up all night. The sun had no chance of peeking through the thick grey clouds today and the morning air was brisk.

As Liz entered the elevator she called for a taxi and sent a text message to Max to update him on where she was headed and why. She had never met Bruce Cunningham. The man had tried to have her killed, to keep his underhanded business dealings secret, but in the end, rich men were hard to pin crimes on.

He'd continued going about his life after Becca's death. Even after the killer was found and the Judge's henchman had been killed by Max, the Judge had come off clean. Not one charge was laid against him, something that irked her until someone tried to poison him.

She'd felt it was karma, until she saw what his father's condition had done to Jack. He'd done everything in his power to find out who had tried to kill his dad. Liz had her suspicions, but hadn't wanted to say anything to Jack until the DNA test had come back. Now she was pretty sure she had the right suspect. Now she could discuss it with Jack, but she needed to talk to Bruce first.

Her phone pinged as the taxi drove up the gravel driveway of the Cunningham family estate. She glanced at the message from Max, warning her that the visit wasn't a good idea, but to call if she needed any help. She sent a message back that she'd meet him for lunch at the pub and to organise Jack to be there. She should have news.

The thumbs up emoji arrived as Liz paid the taxi driver and got out of the car. She heard the tyres crunch on the quartz as the taxi pulled away, leaving her to admire the stone building and sandstone veranda. The gargoyle statue in the middle of the driveway was a nice touch, but it seemed out of place against the Federation building.

Liz walked up the stairs, not really knowing what to expect. Her heart was racing a little as she rang the doorbell. This wasn't how she had hoped to meet Jack's mum. But then, how does a high-class escort really make friends with a doctor and wife of a local magistrate? It wasn't like Jack was ever going to bring her home to meet his mother.

The door opened after what felt like an eternity to Liz. The woman who answered was well dressed, with a small layer of make-up and sensible, yet refined day wear. 'Hello. Can I help you?'

'Yes. I'm a friend of your son's Jack. I consult with the police, may I come in?'

'Oh. He hasn't mentioned you?'

'No, I guess he hasn't.' Liz wondered if Jack spoke about his work at all to his mother. Somehow, she doubted it and took a punt. 'I'm guessing he doesn't talk shop at home often.'

'You are right there dear, come in.' Mrs Cunningham didn't wait to close the door, she led the way, leaving Liz to gently close the door and follow.

'What did you say your name was?' They'd reached the living area and the light that flooded the room belied the winter grey scape outside.

'Her name is Liz.' Bruce's slur from his injuries caught her off guard, but she recovered.

'That's right, I'm Liz Jeffreys, pleased to meet you Mrs Cunningham, Bruce.' She nodded to the man in the wheel chair.

Jack's mum looked from her husband to Liz and frowned, but recovered quickly. 'Can I get you a cup of tea Liz?'

'No thank you Mrs Cunningham.'

'Call me Victoria, please.'

'Thank you. Any chance I can have a chat with Bruce?' She looked at the Judge who nodded to his wife. 'Alone?'

'Whatever you have to say to me, you can say in front of Victoria.' Liz made to protest, but Bruce put his hand up and cut her short. 'Since this happened,' he indicated his chair, 'there's been no secrets between us Ms Jeffreys.' She nodded.

'Maybe I'll take that cup of tea after all Mrs... Victoria.' She smiled and Jack's mum busied herself in the kitchen as Liz took a seat at the Hamptons style dining table in the open plan living area.

Bruce's wheelchair was pulled up to the one end and Liz took the seat alongside. 'You said you're a friend of Jack's. Is this about his case?' Victoria called from the kitchen as the kettle boiled and she poured the hot water into the teapot. Liz smiled at the rather formal British way of making tea.

'Yes and no.' Victoria brought a tray of fine china cups with saucers, cookies and the steaming pot of tea over to the table, placing the cookies close to Bruce. 'It's about both Jack's case and yours Bruce.'

Bruce reached forward, fumbling for a cookie, his hand stopped a moment, suspended as he turned toward at Liz, then picked up the biscuit and took a bite. 'Go on.'

'I wanted to speak with you first. Jack doesn't know, but the rest of the team working on his case does. It turns out the person who tipped off the Task Force about the drugs in Jack's apartment was someone you might know.' She faced Bruce as she spoke and his eyes widened, obviously reconsidering if his wife should be present.

Liz waited, to be sure he hadn't changed his mind. His face regained composure and he nodded for her to continue.

'We believe Narelle Fergusson is the caller and the person who planted the drugs to frame Jack. We were puzzled over her motives until I managed to get a hold of some of her DNA and Jack's partner ran it through a paternity test.

'That's not necessary Ms Jeffreys, I know who Narelle is.' Victoria poured the tea. 'Why would she make a false accusation about Jack like that though?'

'And poison your husband?' Liz offered, taking the cup from Victoria's hand as it began to shake.

'No! How?' She sat down heavily as the doorbell rang.

Liz frowned, pulled her phone out of her pocket and looked to see if Max had changed his mind and decided to butt in after all. The screen was clear. No missed calls or texts. Liz wore the latest *Smart Watch*. She didn't think she could have missed anything, but it un-synced occasionally.

'Are you expecting anyone?' she asked Mrs Cunningham who frowned and looked at Bruce before answering.

'No.' The doorbell rang again.

'Do you have a security system?'

'I never use it.' Victoria got up to answer the door. 'You sound like Jack.' She smiled and moved down the hall.

'You knew Narelle worked at the bar you visited. Is that why you were there?'

She heard a woman's voice down the hall, but she was focussed on the Judge.

'I didn't recognise her. I haven't seen her in decades. Her mother stopped contacting me when she moved to the

Indigenous mission and Narelle ran away.' Liz knew that wasn't entirely true. He'd presided over her solicitation case.

A scream made Liz jump as Bruce tried unsuccessfully to rise from his wheel chair. His legs gave way and he fell back heavily. Liz got up to make sure he was alright but he waved for her to check on Victoria.

'Is everything alright Mrs…' The question didn't need an answer, it was obvious on her face as she came down the hall, a blonde woman holding a gun to her ribcage.

****

'You knock, I'll stand back in case he does anything stupid.' Anderson nodded for Jenny to go ahead. She frowned at his over-reaction, but unclipped her holster, just in case.

She looked for a doorbell, finding nothing, she rapped on the door and stepped back a little, allowing herself some space between the doorway and Rickard.

There was no answer for a moment, but then she heard the sound of someone approaching the door. There was no peephole in the door, but she saw the side window curtain flicker before the latch began to rattle.

'Rickard.' Jenny smiled politely

'Williams. Come to check on me, have you?'

'This is Detective Senior Sergeant Anderson from the Trinity Task Force. He's helping me since Jack's out of the picture at the moment. We need to ask you a few questions.'

'About what?'

'Can we come inside?' Anderson moved forward, holstering his gun in the obvious leg holster he wore over his jeans. He clipped the retention hook back in place as Rickard made room for the detectives to enter.

'I wasn't expecting visitors. No donuts and coffee I'm afraid.' He turned and limped into the house, leaving the door wide open.

'You don't seem surprised to see us?' Jenny looked around as she spoke, still alert and aware that this detective had helped to frame her partner and was likely an accessory to attempted murder.

He took a seat in a worn recliner. Jenny sat on the edge of the three-seater lounge adjacent, while Anderson remained standing, his arms crossed over his chest which he thrust forward even further than his crotch. Jenny hadn't worked with Rickard long. She wasn't sure if he'd be intimidated by Anderson or not. She'd only known him in passing. Friendly rivalry between detectives and not much more. As a probationary junior detective, she felt awkward questioning him in his own home.

Sensing her hesitation, Anderson uncrossed his arms and moved in front of the recliner, looming over the detective ominously.

'You don't need any heavy tactics with me sunshine. I've been around long enough to know the drill.' He stared defiantly at Anderson, then turned his attention to Jenny. 'Johnnie said you were looking for me. I knew you'd turn up sooner or later.'

'He didn't mention you'd hurt your leg.' Jenny continued the interview, a sense of calm and focus pushing her on. Anderson still stood above Rickard, but he moved a little further away when Jenny frowned and gave a slight nod to her right.

'Why would he? I was on sick leave.' He didn't skip a beat.

'How did you hurt the leg?' Jenny pushed.

'I tripped.'

'What, over Jack's balcony?' Jenny snarled and Rickard stiffened.

'You know your best bet is to tell us what you know.' Anderson joined the interview again.

'Actually, my best bet is to call for a lawyer and a police union rep, but I'll humour you for a minute or two. What's this all about?'

'How long have you known Narelle Fergusson?' The name didn't shock him, but the realisation that Anderson knew it sparked his interest. Jenny watched his posture closely. She might have been a country cop, but a big case had gained her an early promotion and she studied hard to make sure she wouldn't be on probation for much longer.

Rickard's cocky posture was gone. He absently rubbed his sore leg and took a deep breath. 'You already know I booked her for solicitation years ago. Why are you looking for Narelle?'

'We could ask you the same question. You were seen by a witness outside her apartment when you were supposed to be on sick leave. On top of that, you've roped Johnnie into trying to chase her down.'

Rickard didn't say a word. He looked at his watch, then the television screen that was not even on, then back to Jenny. 'I need that police rep now.'

30

'We aren't getting anything out of him unless he thinks he needs to make some sort of deal. Everything we have is circumstantial. Even if we arrest Narelle, that isn't exactly going to link him as an accessory.' Jenny slouched in her office chair as Anderson took a seat on the corner of her desk.

Johnnie walked in the door and both detectives eyed him up and down, then looked at one another. Jenny smiled.

'Johnnie, got a second?' She stood up and joined Anderson as they walked to intercept him before he got to his desk.

'I can't talk to you two. Rickard's police union rep and lawyer have told me not to say anything without them present.'

'Really, why do you think that is?' Jenny moved in and Anderson stood back, watching her in action.

She touched his arm gently. He looked at her hand, then up into her eyes. 'I can't Jenny.'

'Johnnie. Someone broke into Jack's apartment, using his key. How do you suppose someone got a copy of his house key?' She linked her arm in his and steered him to his desk. She eased him down into his office chair and sat on the desk directly in front of him.

'I don't know. I'm just a junior detective like you. I just do as I'm told Jenny.' He wrung his hands in his lap and Jenny wondered if he really had it in him to be a Major Crimes detective. He was just too nice.

Anderson stood behind her. She ignored him and channelled Liz. Her right leg sat between his two legs and she let it sway gently from side to side. 'Jack might have left his keys on his desk while he went for coffee. You didn't see Rickard doing something at Jack's desk, did you?' The tone was sweet, she knew. Johnnie's cheeks began to glow slightly red, but as she asked her question, he broke eye contact.

'You did, didn't you? You do know that when we find the evidence, and we will find the evidence, you'll be best off telling us the truth *before* we catch you holding it back.' Her leg continued to sway; his cheeks continued to grow rosier.

'Come on Jen. You're using interview tactics 101 on me. I'm not stupid.' His tone was pleading.

'No!' Jenny pushed his seat back, leaning on the two arm rests and breathing into his flushed face. 'I know you're not stupid which is why you should cough up now, before we charge you with being an accessory. Johnnie, Rickard is involved with a former hooker, a bikie chick who has it in for the Cunningham family. There is a really good chance she tried to kill Jack's dad, frame his mum and get Jack thrown off the force and your partner *has been* an accessory, before the fact. That's premediated attempted murder Johnnie. Then there's Braithwaite's death.'

'I don't know anything. I just drive the car and stay in it while he runs a few errands.'

'You saw him at Jack's desk.'

'It proves nothing.'

'When Johnnie?' She was still leaning on the arms of the chair, still breathing warm air into his face, still making him blush.

'About three weeks ago, around mid-morning. I asked him about it. Came back from the dunny and he was closing Jack's drawer.'

'What did he say?'

'He said he was returning a permanent marker.'

'And you bought it?'

'He's my senior Jenny. I just do as I'm told.'

'Well stop it Johnnie.'

'Am I in trouble?'

'Make me a statement and then you're good to go unless this goes to trial.' Jenny pulled back and physically wheeled Johnnie's chair back to his desk. She yanked a pad from Rickard's desk and thrust a pen into his hand. 'Write.'

He did. Once Jenny had her statement, she turned to see Anderson, a smug grin on his face, his arms still crossed, his tattoos rippling with his bicep muscle. She smiled.

As she walked back to her desk, Anderson followed. 'When did you realise Johnnie might have seen the key copied?'

'Last week, Johnnie wanted to talk to me. I thought it was to ask me out, but he baulked when Rickard came back into the room. It didn't make any sense until just then.'

'You are enjoyable to watch you know. Although, I was a little jealous of him for a second.' He sat on the edge of her desk as she wrote her report.

'Jealous, of the interview?' She got up to take the statement to the scanner.

'The methodology, yes.' She stopped, momentarily speechless.

'You busy for lunch?' The question took Anderson by surprise. He smiled. 'Jack and Max are meeting up with Liz. She went to Jack's dad's place this morning to confront him about being Narelle's dad.'

The smile disappeared. 'And you're telling me this now?'

'Yes. Jack doesn't know yet. Think yourself lucky.' She left to go to the scanner in ops. Anderson shook his head but knew better than to follow her.

Jenny returned and went back to her desk, typing in the name of the file she'd just scanned, so she could find it on the Ops server and add it to her file.

'You going to sit there all morning, or go and do some work?' Jenny didn't take her eyes off the screen, or her hands from the keyboard. Anderson moved to peer over her shoulder.

'I thought I'd hang around here.' She could feel his breath on her right ear, she shivered.

'Look, I'll go over Narelle's file with you now and see if there is a lead to follow. I have paperwork to do, so you can check it out for me.' She went to turn and face him, but stopped. His cheek was close to hers and if she turned, their lips could touch.

'Really? When did I become your PA?'

'When you refused to rack off and find yourself some work to do.' As she turned to face him, she pushed her chair back fast. It struck Anderson in the abdomen. He grunted in surprise, but Jenny knew it wouldn't have hurt. The guy had rock hard abs.

'Okay. Okay.' He held his hands up either side of his head in surrender, turning his hands over as if proving he had no weapon. 'Let's re-check Fergusson's jacket and I'll follow up.'

Jenny turned back to the computer and typed Narelle's details into the Police database. A cursor flashed as the computer searched the files. It felt like an eternity, with Anderson's eyes on her back, but finally the file appeared.

She opened it and scrolled through the prior convictions, checking to see if anyone was arrested with Narelle. 'Her known associates aren't extensive. A few local working girls. A handful of Harlequins members but nothing noteworthy.' She closed the file, then had a thought. 'Hang on a sec, Liz mentioned she had twin adoptive siblings. Give me a second.' Anderson leant forward again, watching the screen as Jenny opened her email account.

She searched for Liz's email address. A list of emails popped up and Jenny hoped Anderson wasn't paying too much attention. Some emails dated back to past cases. She was sure he probably noticed, even though she opened the latest email as quickly as she could.

'Here it is. Nullah and Allyra Fergusson. They have her surname, interesting. They are both at Flinders University but she doesn't have an address for them.'

'I've got a friend at the Uni. I'll see what I can find out.' Anderson pulled out his mobile. 'Coffee?'

'Sure. Just tell the barista in the café downstairs you want my usual.'

'Will do.' He moved toward the doorway and glanced back at Johnnie sitting at his desk. Jenny thought he seemed to be daydreaming, but she saw him glance at Anderson's back as the detective walked out of the office, then he looked at her, his expression hard to read.

'Are you okay?' she asked, suddenly feeling guilty about grilling him.

He shrugged. 'Where is Rickard?'

'Still in holding, waiting charges. He doesn't want to talk yet. We'll see how he goes once we stack up some more evidence. It's not looking good. The earlier he talks, the more he'll help himself.'

'I'll talk to him.'

She wasn't sure if he would listen to his junior partner, but she hoped he would. Jenny attached the video of Jack's B and E to the file she was preparing about Rickard's arrest. She knew they didn't have enough to charge him yet, hold him for questioning, but not charge him. She was hopeful finding Narelle would answer a lot of questions.

'Found them.' Anderson returned, a coffee in each hand. 'Do you really drink this crap?' She grinned; he must have seen the caramel syrup going into her flat white.

'Yes. I'm a sweet tooth, what can I say?' She took the coffee offered and hit *close* on the report.

'Where are we heading? I'm all caught up now.'

'St Marys. The kids live there. They might be on campus, but according to my source, only one has a class on today, so hopefully Allyra is home.'

'What gorgeous names.' Jenny took her weapon out of the drawer, holstered it and grabbed her bag. It was kind of nice not having to drive, since Anderson was unlikely to let her drive his car. The vintage Mustang said a lot about his personality, but she liked it.

A few minutes later, as the midnight blue hot rod roared out of the police underground carpark, she nearly giggled. The engine throbbed enough to make her chest vibrate and heads turned as they accelerated along Angus Street.

31

'Narelle. You don't want to do that.' Liz stood as their assailant shoved Victoria into the dining room hard enough to make her fall and slide along the polished floor.

'Shut up and sit down you bitch.' The gun was waving in all directions and Liz fought the urge to drop to the ground and take cover.

'Okay, I'm sitting. What do you want?' Liz looked at Bruce who tried to speak but the damage done by the poison, together with his sudden rush of adrenalin and fear prevented any words from forming. He reached for Victoria, who was crawling along the ground toward him.

'I want him dead!' The gun pointed threateningly at Bruce, 'her in prison for killing him and that spoilt son of theirs in jail and busted out of the police force. But your interference has fucked everything up.' The gun was pointing at her now.

'That's not going to happen Narelle. Let's talk about *why* you want those things.' Liz kept her voice calm. She'd counselled clients, on the street and in her current business. She had to keep the woman calm, give her an out. 'I saw your mum yesterday.'

'Shut up!' Narelle put her hands to her head as though loud noises were roaring through her brain. Her eye make-up was streaked with tears and the barrel of the gun moved across her right temple, back and forth as she gripped it tightly.

'I've been where you are Narelle.'

'What do you know?' The eyes flew open, glazed and wild.

'I left home at sixteen. Missed my senior year.'

'Lies.'

'It's true. My mum's boyfriend got too friendly. I had no choice.'

'I don't care. Shut up!'

Liz remained silent as Narelle paced back and forth across the dining room and into the kitchen. She decided now was a good time to just let her get her bearings. Hopefully she'd relax and calm down. Then maybe she'd be able to reason with her.

She watched Victoria get to her knees next to Bruce, her hands were shaking, tears were running down her face as she silently sobbed. Bruce held his hand out, helping as best he could. Liz dared not move to help. She needed Narelle to be calm or someone was going to get shot.

She glanced at her watch. It was nearly lunch time. Soon, her phone would ring with either Jack or Max asking where she was. She carefully held her mobile phone through the outside of her jacket. She felt her phone vibrate as it turned off and she slowly let out the breath she'd been holding.

When they got her answering machine, they'd likely call Bruce. That she couldn't stop, but she didn't want Narelle to know she had her mobile on her.

****

Jenny walked into the pub with Anderson alongside her. Jack raised a questioning eyebrow. The look was almost comical and it made her chuckle to herself.

'We found where Narelle has been staying.' She sat down.

'Where?' Jack made to stand up and leave.

'She's gone now. Her adopted sister was worried about her, but Narelle begged her not to call her mum.'

'Why was she worried?'

'Allyra said Narelle was neurotic, like she was strung out on drugs or mentally ill.'

'I'll go with mentally unstable. Her criminal history doesn't say drug addict and she looked pretty clean when Liz and I interviewed her.' Max tapped the menu. 'We eating then?'

'We should wait for Liz,' Jack suggested. 'Any idea where Narelle might have gone?'

'Allyra said she wasn't making any sense. Said she needed to settle a debt. That she had it all planned but someone had mucked it all up. Not her exact words Allyra said, but she didn't use the F word.' Jack chuckled.

Max looked at his watch. 'Liz is late.' He pouted. 'I'm really hungry. Can we order?'

'I'll give her a call.' Jenny was desperate to share the news about Narelle's parentage, but she didn't dare do it until Liz gave the all clear.

She tapped her mobile and put it to her ear as Anderson passed her a copy of the menu. She smiled and started looking it over as the phone rang. It continued to ring until it went to message bank. 'That's weird.'

'No answer?' Jack got his phone out and checked to see if he had a message from Liz. Nothing. 'Try again.'

Jenny did, the call went to message bank.

'Try your mum and dad Jack.' Max had forgotten about his food.

'Why?'

'Long story, she visited your dad this morning. Just check.'

Jack scowled, but he dialled his parents and waited.

****

Victoria had gotten to her seat and was drinking her cold tea, her hands shaking and the tea cup clattering quietly in the saucer between sips. Liz wanted to reach out and touch her, to calm her, but she didn't dare.

They all jumped as the phone began to ring. Liz risked a look at her watch. Her smart watch had its own SIM card and could take calls. She could see the missed call.

'I had best answer that.' Victoria put her cup down with a clatter.

'No!'

'If I don't someone might come over to check. You don't want that do you?' Liz joined the plea.

'Okay, get it, but get rid of them. If I hear anything that sounds like a warning, I'll shoot him.' Narelle pointed the gun at Bruce instinctively. He looked at her tentatively, eventhough his vision was like looking through water.

Victoria reached the phone just as it rang out. Liz could see the woman's shoulders sag as she gripped the side table, trying to compose herself. She was just about to move back to the table when it rang again. She snatched it up. 'Hello.'

'Mum.'

Victoria's hand shook as she tried to compose herself. 'Yes.' She didn't want to say Jack's name out aloud. Narelle was unstable enough, if she heard Jack's name, she'd be enraged.

'Has Liz left?'

'No.' Liz could hear the measured answers. The woman was smart.

'Is everything alright?'

'Bruce is doing alright.'

'Mum, what's going on?'

'I can't talk right now. I need to get Bruce's lunch. Bye for now.' She hung up and stood hovering over the phone. Liz saw her shoulders shudder and went to stand. As the chair slid across the floor, Narelle turned.

'Don't move!'

'I need to help Victoria back to her seat. She's...'

'Shut up!'

'I don't understand Narelle. What's your plan? Keep us here all day until we wet our pants? What do you want?'

'Just shut up and let me think.'

Liz's watch vibrated gently. She kept her hands in her lap as she rolled her wrist to look at the screen. Creating a text from scratch was impossible, given the circumstances, but replying to one was doable. She touched the screen, rolled to a message she'd used once before when she was in trouble. She only hoped Jack would remember.

****

'She's probably fine. You know Liz.' Max fiddled with the menu idly.

'Exactly the reason I'm worried.' Jack's phone buzzed and he glanced down at the screen. 'Fuck. We have to go.'

'What?' Max asked, but Jenny was already grabbing her bag.

'Where?' she asked as Max sighed.

'My parent's place. Mum sounded weird, but this message confirms it. Liz is in trouble.' He showed Max the message.

Now would be good.

'Shit, let's go.'

'What is going on? What's the message?' Anderson followed Jenny out the door even though he had no idea what was going on.

'The message is something Liz sent me when she was in trouble once, when she couldn't use her phone properly.' Jack pushed the double glass doors open and began to jog back to Headquarters and his car.

'Where are you going? My car's just around the corner.' Max called and Jack stopped.

'You don't have a siren and lights.'

'I do, follow me.' Anderson pointed at the midnight blue Mustang and for a second Jenny wasn't sure which car she'd go in. Then she tapped him on the arm.

'I'll see you there.' He nodded, no disappointment in his eyes. He understood. This was her team and she needed to be there for them.

'Kill the sirens before you leave the main road. I don't want to spook whoever has Liz so worried.' Jack called as he followed Max around the corner.

'You got it.'

32

'We need to see what's going on inside.' Jack sat in Max's car across the road from his parent's estate. The binoculars allowed him to see the old VW Passat parked in the driveway. 'I'm sure that's Narelle's car, but run the plate to be sure. Alpha, Romeo, Hotel, Nine, Four, Nine.'

Jenny tapped her screen and called dispatch. 'This is Detective Williams, badge number Six, Five, Two, Seven, Seven. I need a rego check.' She repeated the number and waited, her foot tapping on the front floor of Max's silver Mazda.

'We could call the Hostage Task Force.' Max looked to Anderson who shook his head.

'Not until we are sure we have a hostage situation.'

'Thanks.' Jenny put the phone back in her pocket. 'It's definitely Narelle's car.'

'If Narelle is inside with Liz and my parents. I'm definitely going in.'

'You can't do that Jack. She's unstable and we know she was trying to set you up. She might have a gun. She might shoot you on sight.'

'And she might have already killed my family and Liz. I know a way in. I'll call once I'm inside and give you a report. Then you can call for back up.'

'I'm going with you.' Max moved as Jack started toward the estate. 'No arguments.' His face was set and Jack didn't have time to disagree. He turned and moved along the old stone wall that surrounded the large, city allotment. The wrought iron work offered a good deterrent from intruders with its sharp, spade shaped spikes and narrow spacing.

'How are we getting over?' Max moved behind his ex-partner whispering.

'We have a side gate and I have the key.'

'Convenient.'

'Old staff entrance from back in my grandfather's day.'

'Of course.'

Jack pulled his keyring out of his pocket. 'I just hope the lock hasn't seized or we are climbing over after all.'

'That might prove entertaining.'

'On any other day, it probably would be.' They reached the gate and Jack had the key out, ready to unlock the rusty old padlock. He screwed up his face as he slid the key in. It felt sticky and as he tried to rotate the tumblers, it didn't move. He struggled with it a few times before Max offered to try.

Jack moved aside and Max gripped the key firmly. It didn't look like it was going to budge, then it moved suddenly. 'Got it.' The gate creaked opened and Max swore.

'Over there.' Jack pointed. 'Follow me.' They followed a line of conifer pines, skirting the gravel path and opted for the lawn to keep the noise down.

Max climbed over a short hedge behind Jack and waited, hunched down, gun drawn and ready.

Jack peered over the top, then jumped up. 'All clear. Let's go.' He sprinted across open ground and stopped outside a machinery shed.

'What's this?'

'The pool room.'

Max rolled his eyes but Jack didn't have the time to deal with Max's issues over his family's money. He had nothing to do with it. He'd had nothing to do with his family for years, until recently. Now, he regretted it.

'It leads to the pool, which is covered by the ballroom floor this time of year, but it has a manual override. I can unlock it and we can slide it back far enough to get in.'

'You sure you don't want to check the back door first?'

Jack shook his head. 'Since dad's poisoning, mum has locked every window and every door religiously.'

'Okay, your family, your call mate.'

****

'What do we do now?' Jenny paced alongside Max's car.

'We wait.' Anderson leant against his car casually.

'How are you so calm?'

'Practice. I'm reeling on the inside, believe me. I got you all into this.'

'Liz would have been on the trail of Bruce's poisoner by now regardless. Don't feel too bad. If you call in reinforcements, don't forget to tell them Jack is reinstated.'

'I will. Let's hope we don't need them.'

'What can we use to talk Narelle down?

'Damn. I should have told Jack about Narelle being his half-sister. I can't call him now and texting a message like that just isn't right.'

'You might not have a choice. It might be what Jack needs to talk her off the edge.'

She knew he was right, but texting him didn't seem right. What can she say. *Oh, by the way, your dad slept with a bikie chick and Narelle is his daughter.*

She pulled the phone out of her pocket and started the text. She couldn't send it until he contacted her in case his phone wasn't on silent. Once he sent her a text, she'd know it was safe, but she didn't want to have to type it in a rush.

You need to know, Narelle is Bruce's daughter, your half-sister.

All she could do now was keep an eye on the front door and wait. Or…. A thought came to her. 'Do you know anything about cars?'

'Do.. I.. know.. anything about cars! Is that really a question you need to ask someone who owns this baby?' He caressed the bonnet of his Mustang

'Not every rev-head can fix a car you know.'

'True. What did you have in mind?'

'We need to wait until Jack is settled inside, but see Narelle's car?' Anderson nodded. 'I have an idea. I'm not sure Jack is going to like it, but,' she shrugged.

****

'Narelle, can we talk now?' Liz spoke quietly. Narelle was curled up on the floor, leaning against the end of the kitchen counter like a frightened child. She didn't respond so Liz took that as a yes.

'We all know Bruce is your dad. Why would you want to kill him?'

Still no response. 'When I first found myself on the street I was scared out of my wits. It's a tough gig, running away from home. Why did you leave?'

'I thought my dad might want me. My mum didn't.' The words were barely audible, but Liz looked to see if Bruce had heard. His eyes said he had.

'I've not seen my mum since I left home. I don't know why, shame maybe. Your mum said you used to visit her. That's nice.'

'I did. But when *he* refused to see me,' she stared at Bruce, 'I got messed up.'

'And then you were in his courtroom and he didn't even cut you any slack. I get it.'

Bruce's eyes rose as if to say, *do you know what you are doing?* She could only hope she did.

192

'He doesn't mean to be like he is Narelle.' Victoria's voice was barely above a whisper.

'How long ago did you find out Victoria?' Liz hoped Jack's caring nature came from his mum and not some distant relative.

Jack's mother sucked in a deep breath. 'Only after Bruce came home from hospital.'

'What would you have done if you'd known early?'

Victoria almost cried. 'I would have taken Narelle in. I had no idea. Honey I'm so sorry.' Victoria looked at the distraught woman on the floor of her kitchen and Liz could see she genuinely would have done exactly that.

'Why don't you come to the table Narelle? Put the gun down and we can talk, that's all you really want, isn't it? To tell your story?'

****

Jack and Max braced themselves against the wall and tried not to groan as they manually slid back the electric floor that covered the pool. They clamoured up to the main level and sat against the old stone wall that marked where the original old stone building ended and the addition of the expansive high-ceilinged atrium started.

Jack pulled out his phone as he got to his feet and checked it was on silent before sending the text to say they were in. He and Max moved off toward the kitchen. Seconds later, the phone vibrated to say Jenny had replied. The message made him stop in his tracks so fast, that Max nearly barged into his back.

Max frowned as Jack looked over his shoulder and held up the phone so his ex-partner could see. The former detective opened his mouth in shock as he read, but said nothing, suddenly understanding why Liz wanted to talk to Bruce.

Jack put the phone back in his pocket and signalled for Max to go first, patting where his shoulder holster would normally be. He'd surrendered his service weapon on suspension. Max nodded, pulled his gun once more and moved forward.

They could hear voices as they made their way into the main house from the atrium. The addition to the old homestead was extensive, with the big entertaining area that housed the pool come ballroom. The ballroom led to the huge modern kitchen and two-way butler's pantry, used by catering staff to service the many events his family hosted.

Jack nodded for Max to take the service entrance, as Jack entered the main hallway. He moved past the master bedroom, the guest room and carefully made his way past his father's study. He stopped to listen to the conversation.

He could hear Liz's calm voice. 'What happened after you left home Narelle?'

'I got mixed up with the bikies.'

'The Harlequins?'

'Yep. I knew mum had been a bikie chick and I figured, if she could, why couldn't I? That was a stupid idea, but I knew *he* had connections with them, so what better way to get to know dad, right!'

Jack saw Liz shake her head at his father. She didn't want him to speak. She had Narelle talking and the last thing she wanted was for his dad to put his foot in it.

'Bruce did the wrong thing by you.' His mother was speaking softly now, tears interrupting her words. Jack's heart sank. How could he ever have thought his mother had tried to kill his dad?

Jack gauged his timing. He knew Max would be waiting for the right moment, hidden in the butler's pantry that adjoined the large family kitchen.

'Why did you go after Jack? He's got nothing to do with his dad's shortcomings. You know he's been trying to stop the

Harlequins and organised crime since he discovered Bruce's involvement.' Liz was paving the way for him. Did she know he was there? Maybe she just hoped he was.

'He had everything I didn't. The schooling, the money, the high-society life.' Narelle's tone was agitated and Jack held his breath as his half-sister toyed with the gun on the dining table in front of her.

'Jack rejected it all,' Liz said softly.

'It's true,' his mum offered. She sat alongside Narelle, a chair separating them. Jack ducked into the doorway of his father's study as Narelle looked at his mum.

'You're lying.'

'I wish I was. Jack left home as soon as he left school. He rented our holiday house until he could afford to buy it from us. He paid full market value, refusing to accept it as a gift.' As his mother shared, Jack saw Liz sit back. It was news to her. He'd never fully explained his family situation. There just hadn't been the right time.

'He doesn't see his father, well not until this.' She patted her husband's hand. He wisely stayed quiet.

'You and he have a lot in common.' Liz composed herself again. 'He's stubborn, independent and clever.'

'If I was clever, he'd have died.' She pointed to Bruce.

'Well luckily he isn't or you'd be looking at murder charges. Why not give yourself up Narelle? I can get you a good lawyer. You have grounds for a plea deal. You know a lot about the Harlequins and you've experienced real hardship to this point.'

'I'm not giving myself up.'

'Then what is your plan? Do you really want to kill us all? Me, Victoria here, we had nothing to do with what happened to you as a kid.' Liz's tone stayed calm. The logical argument was reaching Narelle.

He had to give Max a distraction. 'Narelle.' Jack moved out of the shadows, his voice soft, his hands held up to show he had no weapon. The gun was in his half-sister's hand before he could blink. She stood, her body stiff with adrenalin.

'I'm only here to talk.'

'How did you get in?'

'It doesn't matter. I'm here, you wanted us all here didn't you?'

Narelle stared at the faces around the table and slowly sank back down onto her chair. 'I don't know what I wanted. What I thought I wanted.' Her voice drifted from a whisper to almost inaudible.

Jack moved forward. 'Can I join you?' He pointed to the seat next to Liz, opposite Narelle. He needed to get control of the gun before Max could act. He slowly walked toward the table. Narelle nodded. He kept his hands in the air as Liz pulled out the seat next to her and he slowly lowered himself, placing his hands in full sight on the table in front of Narelle.

She moved the gun away, her hand protectively held over the butt and side.

A car engine started in the front yard and Narelle stood, Jack leapt onto the table and grabbed the hand holding the gun.

'What the hell!' Narelle screamed.

'Now!' Jack yelled.

Max appeared, sliding over the kitchen counter with more finesse than an acrobat. He took out two bar stools on the way, both landed heavily against Narelle's back, followed quickly by the large PI.

Jack and Max wrestled Narelle to the ground as a loud roar sounded outside, followed by an explosion of metal and stone. Jack pushed the gun clear as Max clamped Narelle's hands together behind her back. Neither carried cuffs or zip ties, so Max just pinned the woman's wrists together.

Liz appeared seconds later, a scarf in her hand. Jack smiled as he realised it had been around his mother's neck moments ago.

He held out his hand and took it, tying Narelle's hands. 'Thanks Liz. You did good.'

'She did better than good.' Bruce's words were slurred, but loud enough for everyone to hear clearly. Liz turned and studied the man, shaking her head at the praise.

'We wouldn't have been here if you weren't such a jerk. Why didn't you recognise the girl?'

Max lifted Narelle to her feet. 'Now isn't the time Liz.'

'Why not?' Adrenalin had kicked in and Liz's hands were shaking as she pointed her finger at the Judge.

Jack moved forward, placing his hand on her accusing finger. He gently pushed her arm down by her side and stood between her and his father. 'It's okay. You're okay.'

'Why does this shit happen to me all the time?'

Jack smiled as he watched a tear of relief roll down her face. 'Because you are who you are Liz and you find trouble, or trouble finds you.' She took in a deep breath. He wanted to hold her, to hug her to his chest and smooth her hair, but this wasn't the place to do that.

Narelle wasn't struggling. 'Let's get her out of here before special forces storm the house.'

Max grunted and moved Narelle forward toward the front door. Jack looked at his parents. 'I'll be back in a few minutes. Don't touch anything. You know the drill dad.'

Bruce nodded and took Victoria's hand. 'We aren't going anywhere.' His wife stood and embraced the judge, who pulled her onto his lap.

Liz followed Max and Jack as the front door opened and sunlight shone in. The clouds had parted slightly and the morning gloom had eased to reveal an almost sunny afternoon.

As they walked down the steps, Jack spotted the cause of the commotion. Williams and Anderson stood to the side of the gravel driveway, weapons drawn and aimed until they realised Max had Narelle under control.

The wreckage of Narelle's old car was wrapped around the only thing on the estate that he was happy to see broken.

'I'm sorry about that.' Jenny moved forward, holstering her gun. 'I thought you might need a distraction.'

'I won't miss that statue. Your aim was perfect. Did you drive it into that ugly gargoyle yourself?'

'No, we jerry-rigged a pedal jam and steering lock.'

'Nice.' Max offered as he handed Narelle over to Anderson. 'Do you have any real cuffs?'

The Task Force detective looked at the magenta silk scarf and grinned. 'I don't know, I kind of like the touch.' Narelle still wasn't resisting. She looked broken, inside and out.

Liz moved toward her and put a hand on her shoulder as a shot fired. It hit Liz in the shoulder, narrowly missing Narelle. It missed Anderson's head as he was already moving sideways, pulling the two women to the gravel with him.

'Where did that come from?' Jack drew the weapon he'd taken from Narelle. Max pulled his gun clear and both men, together with Jenny scanned the tree line.

Jack heard Jenny's weapon discharge. She was only a few paces behind and to his left, so the bullet whizzed by, making his ears ring.

'Over there. I saw movement. That's where the shot came from.' Jenny pointed her weapon in a two-fisted grip and moved forward at a jog.

'You two check.' Jack ordered and Max joined Jenny in the search. He ran to Liz and the fallen bodies on the gravel. 'Are you okay?'

He rolled Liz clear. She'd landed on top of Narelle and Anderson. The detective managed to lift Narelle from on top of him once Liz was no longer weighing him down.

'I'm fine, just a graze.' Liz held her arm, blood was seeping through her fingers. She saw Jack's face. 'Really, check on Narelle.'

Jack helped Anderson with Narelle. 'You both alright?'

'I'm good.' Anderson answered. Narelle was in shock. Her body was shaking and her eyes were struggling to focus. The whites appeared as she collapsed to the ground.

'Ambulance!' Jack pulled out his phone and started to dial police dispatch.

'I'm following them.' Anderson pointed to Jenny and Max who were going through the bushes trying to find the gunman.

'Go!' Jack agreed as dispatch picked up and he gave them details.

33

'I can see blood. Whoever it was, you got him Jenny.' Max pushed a bush aside.

'Who the hell would want to shoot Liz?'

'I can think of a dozen wives, but I think Narelle was the target. Is Rickard still in custody?'

'As far as I know.'

'Here, more blood.' Max pointed to a small pool of bright red blood as Anderson ran up to join them.

'Let me take the lead. I've got a vest on.'

'You got it.' Max stepped back, and nodded for Jenny to do the same.

The group, with Anderson in the lead walked toward the back of the old stone stables. Anderson rolled around the corner, a shot rang out past his head. As he came to his feet, another shot hit him centre mass, knocking him from his feet.

Max had rounded as the first shot rang out. Anderson hit the ground as Max fired, taking the gunman in the chest. The man staggered, tried to fire again, but Jenny had followed up as Max had ducked and rolled. Her shot took the gunman in the chest again and his legs crumpled out from underneath him.

'What the hell?' Jenny stood with her gun still aimed at the place where Johnnie had stood. She ran to his side, and knelt as life left his eyes.

'Why? Why Johnnie?'

Max leant down and checked Johnnie's pulse before gently pulling Jenny away to face him. 'Williams. Check on Anderson.' She stared at him a moment, but Max's tone and formal use of her name snapped her mind to attention.

Her vision swam as she recalled Anderson going down. 'Hemi. Shit!' She turned and ran back to the detective who was just coming to his feet, the wind knocked out of him. She felt him all over as he smiled lazily.

'A man has to get shot to get your attention.'

'Oh shut up.' Jenny was laughing as she helped him to his feet.

'I think I could do with a beer.'

Max moved to join them. 'I thought Kava was your thing.'

'Well, I think a beer is a little more accessible right now.'

'Not until you've been to the hospital mate.' Sirens sounded in the distance. 'You could have a busted rib or something.'

****

'What did Rickard have to say?' Max asked as he handed Jack a beer.

The fire crackled in the lounge room. Anderson, Jenny, Max and Jack sat on stools along Liz's long sparkling white kitchen bench, watching her fuss around the kitchen.

'He said he broke into my place to steer suspicion away from Johnnie. He wanted to break the lock and cover up that a copy of my key was used. He must have seen Johnnie copying my key.'

'Everything Johnnie told me, was about him, not Rickard. I believed him too. He was so legit.' Jenny took a drink of her beer.

'Rickard hooked Narelle and Johnnie up and felt responsible for what was going on. According to Rickard, Johnnie was doing Narelle's bidding and Rickard was in damage control. Johnnie was his responsibility, at least that's how he felt.'

'So he threw his career away to cover up for Johnnie.' Max shook his head. 'What a dumb arse. Any conclusion on who killed Braithwaite and why?'

'Murder weapon hasn't been found. Narelle admitted to poisoning Bruce and trying to frame Victoria for it. She also gave it up on framing Jack, especially when we showed her the surveillance video, but she seemed really broken up about Braithwaite's death.' Jack took another sip of beer as Jenny picked up the story.

'Then there's the fact Braithwaite was not a light guy and whoever killed him, moved his body. I don't think Narelle could have done that. Johnnie would have been able to, that's for sure and there is no evidence either way, but Rickard could have helped him. Between the two of them, Braithwaite would have been easy to move.'

'I don't think Johnnie was anyone's patsy. I think Narelle might have been doing Johnnie's bidding. From what Jenny has said, he's one fantastic actor.' Liz poked a skewer into the roast pork and began turning the roast vegetables, being careful to keep Hemi's separate from the pork.

'Either way, Johnnie tried to kill her before we could question her.' Max undid the top of his beer and took a seat at the end of the counter.

'Can I get you a wine Liz?' Jack stood and moved to the wine fridge. As he moved past Max, he punched him in the arm for forgetting the host. Max shrugged.

'Yes thanks.' She passed him a wine glass from her top cupboard. 'Dinner won't be long.'

'Did Johnnie really think he could get away with shooting her with three cops and a former detective on scene?' Liz reached for the wine Jack passed over the counter and took a sip.

'Who knows. Maybe it was suicide by cop? Maybe he really thought he'd shoot and run. Either way, it didn't turn out well for him. He was willing to kill Narelle to keep her quiet, so it's pretty easy to see him murdering Braithwaite.' Jack sat back down and took a swig of beer, reaching for a handful of cashew nuts to follow up.

'So how is Narelle doing?' Jenny changed the subject before taking a piece of carrot and dipping it into the basil pesto. She shoved it all in her mouth making further speaking impossible.

'She's undergoing a psych evaluation. I organised her a good lawyer. She's been through hell.' Liz sipped her wine and placed it back on the bench. 'How does it feel to have a sister Jack? No longer the only child,' she grinned.

'I think my mum is kind of happy. She always wanted a daughter.' Laughter erupted, as the tensions eased. The last few days had been hectic, for all of them. 'Seriously, I don't know yet. She did try to kill dad, frame mum and get me kicked off the force.'

'You don't have to worry about that. I've filed my report. You come off like a saint.' Anderson lifted his beer and Max saluted him from the other end of the bench.

'So, is Bruce still part of the Task Force investigation?' Jenny turned to Anderson before reaching for a Jatz cracker and cheese. The detective chuckled at her appetite.

'Bruce is off the hook for now. He's too incapacitated to be of any use to the Harlequins. Maybe Narelle did him a favour? The bikies will likely be lining up a new Judge to put in their pocket.'

'Do we need to put someone on Bruce? Will the Harlequins try to eliminate him because he knows too much?' Max reached for the cashews; Jack pushed the glass bowl closer.

'I don't think so. If I hear anything from our undercovers, I'll let you know, but Bruce has kept his silence all this time. I think they trust him not to blab.'

Liz's phone rang and she moved away from the kitchen, putting a finger in her ear as the joyful conversation volume rose.

'Connie, what's up?'

'Liz. I just got a call from Major Crimes.'

'That's funny, I've got most of them here with me now.'

'It's serious hun. Ted's dead, murdered.'

'What!'

'They found him in his hotel room two nights ago. The police want to speak with you.'

'Me?'

'Yes, they claim you're the last person to see him alive.'

Liz looked at Jack, who had swivelled on his stool when he heard the tone in her voice change.

'They are on their way to bring you in for questioning now.'

The buzzer went on the front door as Liz hung up.

'Do you want me to get that?' Jack asked, not taking his eyes from Liz. She couldn't answer.

What's Next?

I am loving writing this series, but I love keeping in touch with you just as much. I have so much to share and I can often use a little help with cover ideas, advanced readers and even the occasional survey.

Most of all, I want to have the chance to give you even more value with occasional giveaways or great deals from myself and other authors I know.

Book 4 will be out before April 2022, so if you want to be sure not to miss it, keep in touch by joining my readers club. Just visit www.atime2write.com.au or follow me on Facebook or Instagram. Just search for my name.

Books by Fiona Tarr

Foxy Mysteries

Book 1 – Death Beneath the Covers
Book 2 – Presumed Missing
Book 3 – Deadly Deceit
Book 4 – Coming April 2022

Fantasy Books
Covenant of Grace Series

Book 1 – Destiny of Kings
Book 2 – Seed of Hope
Book 3 – Legacy of Power
Book 4 – Heir of Vengeance
Book 5 – The Ehud Dagger – Prequel Novella

The Eternal Realm

Book 1 – The Jericho Prophecy
Book 2 – Delilah and the Dark God
Book 3 – Reign of Retribution

The Priestess Chronicles

Book 1 – Call of the Druids
Book 2 – Relic Seeker
Book 3 – Shiloh Rising
Book 4 – TBA

Printed in Great Britain
by Amazon

46382245R00116